"I can't believe you've lived here three years and we've never met before."

Gold flecks glinted in Bryan's brown eyes as his gaze met hers.

"I guess we travel in different circles," Angela said. "I'm busy with my shop and the theater group—I haven't spent much time in clubs or at parties. And I don't snowboard."

Did that sound dull to him? Maybe she *was* dull, though she preferred to think of it as settled.

"Still, you'd think we would have run into each other before now."

"Maybe we did and you didn't notice me." It wouldn't be the first time a man had looked right past her, to focus on a prettier—and yes, *thinner*—woman.

"No, I would have remembered you." He emphasized the words with a squeeze of her hand and an intense look that sent a tingling sensation clear to her toes.

She'd have remembered him, too. He was exactly the kind of man she always noticed—with dark hair and eyes, an expressive face and an outgoing personality.

Pure leading-man material.

Dear Reader,

When I meet new couples, I like to hear about how they met. There's nothing like a romance story, especially in real life.

I'm particularly fascinated by those stories of unexpected love—the experiences of those who fall hard for people they never thought of as their type. I love these tales where the power of love trumps all expectations or previous experience.

Angela and Bryan, the heroine and hero of *The Man Most Likely,* have that kind of romance, set against the fun, quirky backdrop of Crested Butte, Colorado. I hope you'll enjoy sharing their experience.

I look forward to hearing from readers, so if you have questions or comments about this book, feel free to e-mail me at Cindi@CindiMyers.com or write to me in care of Harlequin Enterprises, Ltd., 225 Duncan Mill Rd, Don Mills, Ontario M3B 3K9, Canada.

Sincerely,

Cindi Myers

The Man Most Likely
CINDI MYERS

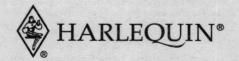

TORONTO • NEW YORK • LONDON
AMSTERDAM • PARIS • SYDNEY • HAMBURG
STOCKHOLM • ATHENS • TOKYO • MILAN • MADRID
PRAGUE • WARSAW • BUDAPEST • AUCKLAND

Recycling programs
for this product may
not exist in your area.

ISBN-13: 978-0-373-75263-8
ISBN-10:   0-373-75263-6

THE MAN MOST LIKELY

This edition published by arrangement with Harlequin Books S.A.

® and TM are trademarks of the publisher. Trademarks indicated with
® are registered in the United States Patent and Trademark Office, the
Canadian Trade Marks Office and in other countries.

www.eHarlequin.com

Printed in U.S.A.

ABOUT THE AUTHOR

The friend who introduced Cindi Myers to her husband swore the man was not her type at all. But from the first moment he and Cindi smiled at each other, something clicked. Six weeks later they were engaged, and they will soon celebrate their thirtieth wedding anniversary. With such a romantic story of her own, how could Cindi not write romance stories—especially about those who find love where they least expect it.

Books by Cindi Myers

HARLEQUIN AMERICAN ROMANCE
1182—MARRIAGE ON HER MIND
1199—THE RIGHT MR. WRONG

HARLEQUIN SUPERROMANCE
1498—A SOLDIER COMES HOME
1530—A MAN TO RELY ON
1549—CHILD'S PLAY

HARLEQUIN NEXT
MY BACKWARDS LIFE
THE BIRDMAN'S DAUGHTER

HARLEQUIN SIGNATURE SELECT
LEARNING CURVES
BOOTCAMP
  "Flirting with an Old Flame"

HARLEQUIN ANTHOLOGY
A WEDDING IN PARIS
  "Picture Perfect"

Don't miss any of our special offers. Write to us at the following address for information on our newest releases.

Harlequin Reader Service
U.S.: 3010 Walden Ave., P.O. Box 1325, Buffalo, NY 14269
Canadian: P.O. Box 609, Fort Erie, Ont. L2A 5X3

To Connie, who introduced me to my husband.
You did good!

Chapter One

"So, Mr. Perry—Bryan—what are your thoughts on chocolate?"

The question, and the throaty, velvety tones in which it was delivered, caught Bryan Perry, new assistant manager of the Elevation Hotel at Crested Butte Mountain Resort, off guard. He sat back in his chair behind his desk in the hotel offices and stretched his legs out in front of him. This voice was worth getting comfortable and savoring, even if the woman it belonged to—one Angela Krizova—did ask strange questions. "I haven't thought much about chocolate," he answered.

"Then you haven't tasted *my* chocolates."

The sexy purr did things to his insides. Who *was* this goddess and how had he lived in Crested Butte for seven years without encountering her? "Are you offering samples?" The remark popped out before he could censor it. Thank God his manager, Carl Phelps, wasn't within hearing range. He'd probably see this mild flirtation as yet another reminder that Bryan, until recently a part-time night auditor and full-time ski bum, was not exactly management material.

"That could be arranged," Angela said smoothly. "We should probably get together anyway."

Bryan's heart sped up in anticipation. Being attracted to a woman based solely on her voice was a new experience for him, but anyone who *sounded* this sexy was bound to be the woman of his dreams. "I'd like that," he said, doing his best to imbue the words with some sex appeal of his own.

"I need to look over the ballroom, and we can discuss decorations and other refreshments for the fund-raiser," Angela said.

Right. The community theater fund-raiser. The whole reason behind this conversation. He sat up straight again, reality cooling his fantasies. "Good idea. What day works for you?" He pretended to study his desk planner, though all he really saw was the vision of a sultry blonde—or brunette, he wasn't picky—that Angela's voice had conjured.

"How about tomorrow afternoon? I have a girl who works part-time in my shop then."

"Which shop is that?" he asked, partly to refresh his memory and partly to keep the woman on the line. That voice…

"The Chocolate Moose. On Elk Avenue."

Bryan nodded. Crested Butte's main street was lined with candy-colored Victorian era and replica-Victorian buildings that catered to locals and tourists alike. Not having a big sweet tooth, he'd never been inside the Chocolate Moose. Now maybe that would change.

"I asked about chocolate because, while I know the hotel usually supplies the catering for these events, I want to provide a selection of desserts from my shop," Angela continued. "You can provide everything else, but I want to be in charge of chocolate."

Company policy, which Phelps had drummed into Bryan's head daily since his first hour on the job, stated that no outside food was to be brought into the hotel for special events. But hey, the woman was a chocolate specialist, and what Phelps didn't know... "I'm sure that won't be a problem," Bryan said.

"Great. Why don't I meet you at the hotel tomorrow afternoon? About three o'clock?"

"Great. I'll look forward to it." Bryan was still smiling when he hung up the phone.

"You really need to lay off the 900 numbers during working hours, dude."

He looked up and suppressed a groan as his best friend, a snowboarder who went by a single name, Zephyr, sauntered into the office. Dressed in black-and-orange camo boarding pants and jacket, the ends of his blond dreadlocks damp from snow, Zephyr contrasted alarmingly with the pale mauve walls and elegant cherry furniture of the hotel offices. "I was talking with a client," Bryan said.

"A sexy, female client from the look on your face." Zephyr sat on the corner of Bryan's desk, shoving aside a stapler and a stack of memo pads to make room for his rear end. "I guess every job has its perks, even this one."

"Yeah, perks like a regular paycheck," Bryan said.

Zephyr snorted. "I guess I'm just not a regular paycheck kind of guy. I prefer to live more on the edge."

"That's because you have a girlfriend who supports you." Zephyr's girlfriend, Trish, owned a successful coffee shop on Elk Avenue.

"Hey, I contribute. Besides, Trish is the kind of woman who *needs* to take care of someone. I'm helping her fulfill her destiny."

Bryan grinned. "Who would have thought you'd be anyone's destiny?"

"So truth, dude, how's it going?" Zephyr looked around the office. "This looks like a really stuffy scene."

"It's not so bad," Bryan said. "And it feels good to finally be putting all that expensive education to work."

"A college education is never wasted. At least that's what I always tell my parents. Anyway, I never saw you as a management type. The whole all-work-and-no-play thing is such a drag."

"Hey, I'm still me," Bryan protested. "Just me who can afford to eat something better than ramen noodles five nights a week. And me with better clothes." He smoothed the lapels of the suit, for which he'd paid extra to have tailored to a custom fit.

"Clothes, but not style." Zephyr adjusted his parka. "Only a few of us really know how to wear clothes."

"Bryan, did you make those phone calls I asked you to make?"

Bryan straightened as Carl Phelps, the manager of the Elevation Hotel, entered the office. Carl stared at Zephyr, one eyebrow raised in question. "Is this a friend of yours?" he asked.

"He was just leaving." Bryan shoved Zephyr off the corner of the desk.

Zephyr landed on his feet and strode toward Carl, hand outstretched. "I'm Zephyr," he said. "I'm here scouting locations for my new cable television show, *The Z Hour.* Maybe you've heard of it?"

Carl slowly shook his head.

Zephyr did a three-sixty turn. "This place has possibilities. I could see setting up the cameras in the lobby, maybe doing a little feature."

Carl stared at Bryan over Zephyr's shoulder, silently telegraphing the question, *Is this guy for real?* Bryan managed a smile and a nod. Zephyr was real, all right; he just made his own reality.

"It was great to meet you." Zephyr grabbed Carl's hand and pumped it. "We'll talk later. I'll have my people call your people. We'll do lunch." He strolled out of the office, pausing to collect a mint from a bowl on the credenza by the door.

Bryan sank back in his chair, suppressing a grin. Nothing like a visit from Zephyr to liven up a dull afternoon.

"Did you take care of those phone calls?" Carl asked.

"Oh, yeah. Yes, sir." Bryan moved the stapler and memo pads back into place. "The contractor will be in to repair the dining room window on Monday, and I'm meeting with Ms. Krizova tomorrow afternoon about the community theater fund-raiser." A meeting that would no doubt be the highlight of his day. Maybe his week.

"Good." Carl sat in the chair across from Brian's desk. "You're doing a fine job." He glanced toward the door. "Was your friend serious? Does he really have a television show?"

"He does. It's sort of a talk show–local affairs thing he started this summer. So far it's been really successful." That was the thing about Zephyr—he looked and acted like a bum, but there was a real brain underneath that shaggy hair, and he had the personality to carry off anything.

Bryan was more reserved and lately, the take-life-as-it-comes philosophy hadn't been very satisfying. He was ready to go out and make things happen, hence the decision to trade in his ripped jeans and knit caps for a suit and tie and finally use the degree he'd earned seven years earlier. The day after attending his third wedding of the summer, he'd awakened in the morning and realized he was ready to grow up. He wanted the whole picture—the steady job, the house, the wife and kids, everything.

In some ways, it was the most radical thing he'd ever done. And one of the hardest.

"I suppose appearing on that kind of show could be good publicity," Carl said. "What do you think?"

Bryan considered the question. "It would be good," he said. "Zephyr pulls in a pretty diverse audience, plus the hotel could benefit from the exposure. It would help us seem more a part of the community, instead of some big corporate interloper." The Elevation was relatively new on the Crested Butte scene; Carl had arrived only a month before hiring Bryan.

"Exactly." Carl nodded. "You've got the instincts I was looking for when I hired you." He leaned back in his chair, hands folded on his stomach. "There were people here who had their doubts, considering your lack of experience, but I have a good sense for these things."

"I appreciate you giving me a chance," Bryan said. If only other people would be more willing to see him differently. He'd heard some of his friends had actually made bets on how long he'd last in this new lifestyle.

"This theater fund-raiser is exactly the sort of community function I hope we'll do more of," Carl continued. "I'm counting on you to see that it all goes smoothly."

"I'm looking forward to it." It didn't hurt that sultry-voiced Angela Krizova was his liaison with the theater group. She'd sounded young and sexy on the phone, and she had her own successful business. Zephyr might give him a hard time about being all work and no play, but Bryan wasn't opposed to mixing business with pleasure, especially where an appealing woman was concerned. Maybe Angela was the ideal woman for a young professional on his way up.

"LET ME GUESS. You couldn't afford a beach vacation, so you decided to make your own."

Angela Krizova looked up from the work table behind the front counter of the Chocolate Moose at her friend from the Mountain Theatre, Tanya Bledso, who had just come in from the snowstorm raging outside. Angela adjusted the silk orchid she'd tucked behind her left ear, wiped her hands on her Hawaiian print apron, and gave a hula shimmy as she went to greet her friend. "If I can't get to paradise, then paradise can come to me," she said. "What do you think?"

Tanya unwound a pink woolen scarf from around her throat and looked around at the candy shop turned tropical escape. Jimmy Buffett crooned in the background and the four tables in front were covered in tropical-print fabric and strewn with silk flowers. A placard by the cash register announced a special on macadamia nut truffles, and the stuffed moose head on the back wall wore sunglasses and a colorful lei. With the heat turned up to seventy-five, condensation had formed on the front windows, obscuring the sight of winter.

"Nice," Tanya said at last. "Can I stay here until June?"

"Next week I may decide I feel like traveling to Scotland, but this week, it's Hawaii comes to Elk Avenue," Angela said. "Tell all your friends." She moved back behind the counter. "What can I get you?"

"I was going to ask for hot chocolate, but it seems inappropriate now." Tanya sat at one of the tables, her gloves, parka, scarf and hat piled in a chair beside her.

"How about a non-alcoholic chocolate colada and a couple of the chocolate gingersnaps I just pulled out of the oven?"

"Sounds heavenly. And fattening." Tanya made a face. "I'll try a small one."

"One more reason I'm glad I'm not a leading lady,"

Angela said as she dumped coconut milk, pineapple juice and chocolate syrup into a blender. "Nobody cares if the heroine's sidekick wears a size sixteen." Besides, if she'd been that concerned with being skinny, she wouldn't have started a business that required dealing with sugar, cream, butter and other luscious ingredients all day.

"You're the best sidekick I ever had," Tanya said. "You can act rings around some of the people I worked with in L.A."

"Can we print that in the playbill of the next Mountain Theatre production?" Angela splashed skim milk into the blender and added a scoop of ice. "Former Hollywood star says Crested Butte actress has talent."

"I wasn't a star." Tanya raised her voice to be heard over the roar of the blender. "That's why I came back to C.B. Annie and I were practically starving to death in L.A."

"I'm sure glad you came back." Angela poured the drink into a malt glass, added a cherry and a straw. "The theater has a whole new life since you showed up." And since the Mountain Theatre was a big part of her life, she was doubly grateful to Tanya for her role in revitalizing the troupe.

"I've had help," Tanya said. "Your idea to have a chocolate extravaganza for a fund-raiser was great." She accepted the drink and took a long pull at the straw. "Wow. You've got to put this on the menu for the fund-raiser. With rum. How's that coming, by the way?"

"This afternoon I spoke with a guy at the Elevation Hotel who's supposed to help coordinate everything." Angela smiled at the memory of the flirtatious conversation. When she'd contacted the hotel and been told the assistant manager would call her back she'd expected to hear from some older stuffed shirt, not a young-sounding, sexy guy.

"What's his name?"

"Bryan Perry." A name she wouldn't forget any time soon. "I don't know him." But she was definitely looking forward to meeting him. She wanted to see if the real man lived up to her telephone fantasies.

"You need to get out more," Tanya said. "Or see someone besides theater people."

"I like all kinds of people. It's just that between this shop and the theater, I don't have a lot of time." She sat across from Tanya and helped herself to one of the chocolate gingersnaps. They were baked from a new recipe she'd developed, and if she did say so herself, they were delicious. "Do *you* know Bryan?" she asked.

"I know *of* him." Tanya reached for a cookie. "He's one of those guys this town is full of—good-looking, fun and totally irresponsible."

Okay, she'd already pictured the cute and fun part, but irresponsible? "A guy like that is in charge of our fund-raiser at the hotel? That doesn't sound good."

"That *is* strange," Angela agreed. "I didn't even know he had a job. But he's a nice guy."

"Wait a minute." She studied Tanya more closely. "Have you dated him?"

Tanya shook her head. "Not me. Divorced women with kids do not attract party guys like that. But I've seen him around. I can't believe you haven't. You've been here, what, almost three years? And I've only been back in town a few months."

Angela nodded. "Yeah, but if he doesn't buy chocolate or hang out at the theater, he's not on my radar. Though maybe I should expand my horizons a little."

"This fund-raiser might be the excuse to get to know him better."

"Maybe." Flirting with a guy over the phone was a long

way from starting a real relationship—something she'd successfully avoided for three years now.

"Not interested in settling down?" Tanya sighed. "I can't say it worked out all that well for me. Of course, I did get Annie out of the marriage. But she's about the only high point of an otherwise wasted seven years."

It wasn't that Angela was opposed to love and marriage and happily-ever-after—at least in movies, plays and books. But in real life she felt safer remaining on her own, rather than getting her heart stomped on when she didn't live up to some guy's idea of Ms. Right.

In any case, Bryan probably had his pick of women if he was the type of guy who filled this town. The best she could hope for when they met was more mild flirtation and fuel for her private fantasies. And that was more than enough until she found a man she could count on to be there for her. Always.

"BRYAN, MS. KRIZOVA is here to see you."

Bryan startled, awakening from an expense-report-induced doze. He leaned forward and depressed the intercom button. "Tell her I'll be right there." Anticipating this appointment had gotten him through a morning filled with dull meetings and even duller reports. He smoothed his tie, buttoned his jacket, then went out to greet his visitor.

February was one of the busiest months at the ski resort and the lobby was packed. As Bryan scanned the cavernous room, he quickly ruled out anyone dressed for the slopes, as well as two mothers with young children and all the men. That left a hefty brunette in a wine velvet dress, black leather boots and a low-slung black leather belt at the front desk, and a petite blonde in gray tweeds by the fire. Neither was the bombshell Angela's voice had led him to expect, but the blonde had definite possibilities.

He started toward the blonde, but froze when a familiar voice spoke behind him. "Mr. Perry?"

He turned to face the brunette, smiling to cover the sudden sick feeling in his stomach. This was the voice that had wowed him over the phone, all right, but this was not the woman he'd pictured. "I'm Angela Krizova," she said, offering her hand.

He took it, the dulcet tones of her words rolling over him. Her hand was warm and soft, and up close he could see she had jade-green eyes and a generous mouth. In fact, everything about her was generous—overly generous. He swallowed hard. Angela Krizova was, well, *fat*. Definitely *not* the woman of his dreams.

She withdrew her hand, looking amused. "Not what you expected?" she asked.

He cleared his throat to cover his embarrassment at allowing his feelings to be so transparent. "Excuse me?"

"I asked if I was not what you expected. Don't worry, I'm used to it."

She turned to survey the lobby and he closed his eyes, collecting himself.

"Nice place you have here," she said, the same sweet, velvety voice wrapping around him. "I haven't been here since it was redone."

He opened his eyes again, half hoping to see the woman of his fantasies. Nope. Angela still stood before him, larger than life—or at least larger than he'd expected. He realized she was studying him, waiting for him to speak. "Let me show you around," he said.

He led her through the lobby toward the restaurant decorated in dark wood and light stone. "The Atmosphere Restaurant and Bar has a sundeck with a fire pit right at the base of the ski slopes. We also have the Cirrus Lobby Bar. And down this hallway is our business center and indoor heated pool and spa." He started to feel more comfortable. He'd given this same talk so many times he could practically say it in his sleep. Which was just as well, since while his tongue was otherwise engaged, every other sense was focused on the woman beside him.

Now that he'd recovered from his initial shock, he felt a little ashamed of his reaction to her. Yes, she was a big woman, but she wasn't ugly. She had thick, lustrous dark hair that fell past her shoulders; expressive eyes, high cheekbones and a Cupid's bow mouth; and her curves, though generous, were in all the right places. Some people might even say she was voluptuous rather than fat.

"May I see the ballroom where we'll be holding the fundraiser?" she asked.

"Of course." He paged the catering manager and asked him to meet them there. Then he led the way into the ballroom and pressed the switches that flooded the room with light. "We can set up tables in any one of several configurations," he said as they walked farther into the room. "The raised dais at the end can be used for speakers or a band or you could showcase silent-auction items there."

"We can put the silent-auction items opposite the entrance and have tables set up along the sides. We'll definitely want room for dancing," she said. "And will there be a coat check available?"

"Yes, we can arrange for that, no problem."

"That would be perfect." Her smile, in conjunction with

that killer voice, would have stopped any conscious man in his tracks.

Bryan took a deep breath, trying to steady himself, but the scent of Angela's subtle floral perfume wrapped around him, further dazzling his senses. Forget the two-dimensional fantasies he'd conjured earlier. The flesh-and-blood woman before him had his expectations—and his libido—in a tailspin. Was he merely responding to the novelty of a plus-size siren, or was there something else at work here?

A stocky man with closely cropped black hair bustled into the room. "I am Marco Casale, the catering manager," he said.

"Marco, this is Angela Krizova. She'll be working with you to arrange the community theater fund-raiser."

Marco took one of Angela's hands in both of his and fixed her with a dazzling smile. "It's a pleasure to meet you, Ms. Krizova," he said. "You perhaps do not remember me, but we spoke several months ago regarding a special order of chocolates you created for a wedding I catered."

"Of course I remember."

Marco's eyes glazed slightly as Angela's voice worked its magic, and Bryan felt a completely unexpected pinch of jealousy in his gut. He hadn't realized quite how much he'd enjoyed being the focus of Angela's attention until he had to share it with another man.

Marco moved in closer, still holding her hand. "We should meet privately sometime soon to discuss the menu for your gathering," he said, his Italian accent more pronounced than usual. "I have some special dishes I have been saving."

"That's great. Why don't you fax her a menu?" Bryan clamped his hand on Marco's shoulder. "Don't let us keep you. I know you have a lot of work to do." Their eyes met in the kind of mute challenge men engage in when physical dueling would be crossing the line into outright incivility.

Marco was the first to blink, and with obvious reluctance released his hold on Angela and backed away. "I will call you," he said to Angela, before sending a last withering look toward Bryan and leaving.

Angela watched his departure, the dimple to the left of her mouth deepening as her lips curved in a hint of a smile. When she and Bryan were alone again, she turned to him. "I almost forgot this," she said as she opened her purse and took out a small, gold foil box.

"What is that?" he asked, watching her untie the ribbon that secured the box lid.

"I brought samples."

"Samples?"

"Of my chocolates." She selected a truffle from the box and held it up for his inspection, the shiny pink lacquer of her nails contrasting sharply with the velvety blackness of the sweet. "Dark chocolate raspberry," she said, and offered it to him.

He popped the confection into his mouth and was instantly rewarded with the smooth sensation of melting chocolate, the bitterness of the cocoa and the sweetness of the raspberries in perfect harmony. "Delicious," he mumbled.

"I'm glad you like it." She licked the tip of her index finger, where the heat of her body had melted the fragile chocolate. The innocent, unself-conscious gesture sent a jolt of arousal straight through him, rocking him back on his heels. Then she smiled at him and said in that voice, "Would you like another?"

Could I survive another? "Maybe you could leave them for me to enjoy later," he said.

"Of course." She replaced the lid on the box and handed it to him. "How long have you been working for the hotel?"

"Not very long." The last he'd heard, the oddsmakers in town had given him three months before he cried uncle and fled to his former slacker ways. He'd passed that mark two weeks ago, but they still treated his new career as a passing fancy, something he was bound to give up on sooner rather than later.

"And what did you do before that?"

"Different things," he hedged. Of course, if she was really interested, five minutes spent talking to any of his friends would give her the full, if not necessarily flattering, picture of his past. He'd arrived in Crested Butte seven years ago this month, intending to spend the rest of the winter snowboarding before heading to New York or Chicago or Dallas to put his hotel management degree to use.

As soon as he'd pulled onto Crested Butte's snow-packed main drag and seen the funky shops and even funkier people, he'd gone into a kind of trance from which he'd only recently awakened. "How long have you had your candy shop?" he asked, anxious to change the subject.

"Three years," she answered. "The first night I was here I tried to buy chocolate and the only thing I could find was a two-month-old Hershey's bar. I knew then I'd found my destiny."

He was amazed she'd known so quickly what she wanted to do, while it had taken him years to figure it out. She had an air of confidence and serenity he hadn't seen in most of the more conventionally beautiful women he'd dated.

"Is something wrong?"

The question made him realize he'd been staring at her. He looked away and reminded himself of the reason they were standing here in the first place. "How many people do you expect to attend?" he asked.

"About a hundred and fifty. We're charging fifty-five dollars each or a hundred dollars a couple for tickets. There will be a silent auction as well as food, a cash bar, music and dancing. And chocolate, of course."

"Of course." He returned her smile. She had a great smile, one that radiated her enjoyment of the moment. "It sounds like fun."

"I hope you'll join us," she said. "There'll be a lot of local people there." They left the ballroom and started toward the front lobby. "Have you seen any of our productions?"

He admitted he had not. Until recently, theater tickets weren't part of his budget or his scope of interest.

"We're rehearsing now for *I Hate Hamlet*," she said. "We're always looking for volunteers and it's a great way to meet new people."

"Maybe I'll do that."

"Our next rehearsal is tomorrow night. We meet at the Mallardi Cabaret, upstairs from the Paragon Galleries, at Second and Elk. You ought to stop by."

They paused near the front desk. "Thanks for the chocolates," he said. "It was good to meet you."

"Thank you. It was a pleasure meeting you." She gave his hand an extra squeeze on the word *pleasure*. Struck dumb, he stared after her as she sashayed across the lobby and out the door. Several heads turned to watch her departure. She may not have been skinny, but Angela definitely had style.

"It looks like Ms. Krizova's been sampling a few too many of her own creations."

He turned and saw the hotel receptionist standing at his elbow. Rachel was about his age, slim and stylish and part of the crowd of young people who frequented the clubs around town. He usually enjoyed talking to her, but the catty remark about Angela rubbed him the wrong way. No matter that he'd thought much the same thing when he first laid eyes on her. Half an hour in her company had given him a different impression entirely. "Did you need me for something?" he asked.

She arched one carefully plucked eyebrow at his brusque tone. "The Chamber of Commerce called about a donation for the Al Johnson Memorial Ski Race," she said. "Mr. Phelps said you'd take care of it."

"Sure." He took the memorandum from her and turned toward his office.

"Some of us are meeting up at LoBar tomorrow night," she said. "There's a new band playing, so we thought we'd check them out. Want to come?"

Even an hour ago, he would have jumped at the chance, but now the invitation held little attraction. "Sorry, I've got other plans."

She leaned toward him, her tone flirtatious once more. "What are you doing that's more fun than going out with me and my friends?"

"I promised to stop by the community theater group." He cleared his throat. "It's business."

She looked toward the door Angela had exited. "Uh-huh." Then she turned back to him, her smile brighter than ever. "Too bad. You'd have a lot more fun with me and my friends. Nobody in that theater group is really your type."

His type. How could she be so sure what his type was when he didn't even know himself? He glanced at Rachel again, taking in her trim figure, glossy hair and dazzling smile. *She* was the sort of woman he usually dated. The type most men preferred. All he had to do was turn on the television or pick up a magazine to know that. Angela must have put him into some chocolate-induced trance to have him thinking otherwise.

"Of course she—I mean the theater group—really isn't my type." Carl had encouraged him to foster connections between the hotel and the community, so that's what he'd be doing.

"It's just business," he said, and retreated to his office.

Chapter Two

Angela settled into a front-row seat at the Mallardi Cabaret, home to Crested Butte's Mountain Theatre group, and pulled out her copy of the script for *I Hate Hamlet*. Around her, other cast and crew members congregated, sipping coffee, discussing the latest snowfall totals, their plans for the upcoming Al Johnson Memorial Ski Race or bemoaning the number of weeks until softball season began. Angela smiled, reveling in the homey familiarity of the scene. Once upon a time she'd dreamed of being a professional actress, but the daunting reality of competing for professional jobs in Los Angeles or New York had convinced her she was better off sticking close to home. She didn't make her living on the stage, but outside her candy shop, her life revolved around the dusty velvet seats and greasepaint-scented air of community theater.

She opened the script and turned to her lines for the scene that was first up on the rehearsal schedule. She played the agent, Lillian Troy. Lillian's claim to fame was that she had once had an affair with the late John Barrymore. Angela's friend Tanya played Felicia, the glamorous girlfriend of the male lead, Andy, who was played by local heartthrob Austin Davies.

At that moment, the man himself crossed in front of Angela. Dressed casually in jeans and a fleece henley, his hair perfectly styled, his jaw perfectly rugged, Austin was the very picture of the leading man. He was a nice enough guy—vain without being obnoxious, over-confident about his abilities at times, but a decent actor.

He smiled at Angela and she nodded, then ducked her head and pretended renewed interest in her script. She wasn't interested in being overly friendly with Austin. The truth was he reminded her a little too much of Troy Wakefield, the leading man in the community theater group she'd belonged to in Broomfield, Colorado, where she'd lived before moving to Crested Butte. The man she'd been engaged to for fifteen minutes.

Okay, more like fifteen days. Same difference for all she'd mattered to Troy. Old news that really didn't concern her anymore.

She looked around to see who else was here. She spotted Tanya on the far side of the stage, running over her lines with Alex Pierce, the older man who was playing Barrymore's ghost. Though tonight she was dressed like everyone else in jeans and a sweater, Tanya's costume for the play was a short, tight, sparkly cocktail dress that showed off her perfect figure. With her red hair teased into waves that tumbled about her shoulders, she'd be the picture of the glamorous femme fatale.

Angela, meanwhile, would be stuck in a frumpy tweed skirt, no-nonsense sweater set and makeup designed to make her look thirty years older.

Just once it would have been fun to play the glamour girl, but she'd never been given the opportunity and probably never would.

"All right, places everyone." Tanya called everyone to order. "Let's run through the séance scene."

Angela, Tanya and Austin gathered center stage around a white-draped table while Alex waited in the wings for his cue. Scripts in hand, they began the run-through of the scene in which the three friends try to contact the ghost of John Barrymore.

But instead of the late, great actor showing up on cue, the door to the theater opened, letting in the sounds of traffic on Elk Avenue below and a man in a dark overcoat. "Um, sorry," he called as he pulled off his gloves. "I didn't mean to interrupt."

"Bryan! You came to see us after all." Angela didn't try to hide her delight. And she couldn't ignore the way her heart sped up at the sight of him.

Tanya gave her a speculative look, then turned to Bryan. "Why don't you have a seat down front," she said. "We'll take a break when we're done with this scene. Angela, I think it's your line."

Angela forced her attention back to the script, trying to forget about the man seated only a few feet away and to put herself back into the character of the sixty-year-old woman recalling her glory days.

She got through it somehow and trooped off the stage with everyone else when they were done. Bryan stood as she approached his seat, the same front-row spot she'd occupied earlier. "That was great," he said.

She smiled, determined to play it cool and not let him see how much his presence flustered her. She hadn't really expected him to take her up on her invitation to visit, not after the mixed signals he'd sent during their meeting. "It's a pretty funny play," she said.

"No, I mean you were great," he said. His eyes locked on to hers. She read definite interest there and struggled to quell the sudden uprising of butterflies in her stomach.

"Thank you. And thanks for coming tonight."

"Hey, Bryan." Austin joined them. "What brings you here? Decided to add acting to your list of new interests?"

"Angela and I are working together on the fund-raiser," Bryan said. "I thought it would be a good idea to meet some of the other people involved."

"Oh, business." Austin looked sympathetic. "I'm sure you'd much rather be over at LoBar."

"No, I'm interested in learning more about the group and what you do."

Angela thought Bryan sounded annoyed. Austin did have that effect on some people.

"Hello, Bryan." Tanya squeezed in next to Angela. "It's good to see you."

"Good to see you, too." He nodded to Tanya, and Angela waited for the inevitable. Whenever she and Tanya were together, every man in the room focused his attention on Tanya and forgot Angela existed. They couldn't seem to help themselves. It had happened so often, it didn't even bother Angela anymore.

Much.

But, while Bryan was friendly toward Tanya and listened to her explanation of the play and the makeup of the theater group and their plans for the money from the fund-raiser, his eyes didn't assume the slightly feverish look so many men's did in her presence.

"We have forty or fifty people involved in the group off and on, depending on the size of the production," Tanya said. "Crested Butte has had a community theater for over thirty-five years now, though I've only taken over as director recently."

"It sounds like a great group," Bryan said. "I'm glad Angela invited me to stop by."

Tanya checked her watch. "We need to run through the next scene, but you're welcome to stay and watch," she said.

The next scene featured only Tanya and Austin, so Angela settled beside Bryan to watch. As usual, Tanya lit up the stage. For ten years prior to returning to Crested Butte, she'd worked in Los Angeles, acting in commercials. She even had a part in a popular soap opera for a while. She'd been a professional and her skill showed. When she spoke her lines, the audience was transported to that New York City apartment where the play was set.

When the scene ended, everyone applauded. "She's brilliant," Angela said. "We're so lucky to have her back, with all her talent and experience."

"I'm no expert, but you seemed every bit as good to me," Bryan said. "Aren't you the star, or the female lead, or whatever it's called?"

She laughed. "You flatter me. No, I am *not* the star. That's Tanya. I'm the supporting actress. The comic relief."

"If the rest of the play is like the little bit I saw, you'll steal the show."

"Thanks." She looked away, trying not to show how flustered she felt. Why would he go out of his way to flatter her so? After their meeting at the hotel, she'd asked a few people about him—very casually, under the pretext of wanting to know more about the man she'd be working with. Women invariably described him as good-looking and fun. Men said he was a good softball player and snowboarder.

"Hey, Bryan! What's up?" Chad, one of the crew members who helped with set construction, emerged from backstage and headed for them. He and Bryan bumped fists. "I been missing you on the slopes," Chad said.

"I've been busy," Bryan said.

"Yeah. I heard you were working at the hotel." Chad shoved his hands in his pockets. "What's up with that? I hear you're even, like, a manager or something."

Bryan flushed. "I have a degree in hotel management. Decided it was time I put it to good use."

Chad laughed. "Never thought I'd see the day you'd go over to the other side," he said.

"What other side?" Angela asked.

"The suit-and-tie corporate side," Chad said. "This guy—" he put his hand on Bryan's shoulder "—was one of the slacker kings. He and his buddy Zephyr showed us all how it was done." He shook his head. "I can't believe you gave up all that freedom for some job."

Bryan shrugged off Chad's hand. "I guess I figured it was time I grew up."

"Oh, I'm wounded." Chad clutched at his chest dramatically. "That hurts, bro."

Bryan, a slacker? Angela considered the idea. It was true the picture his friends had painted didn't exactly fit with the polished professional image he'd presented to her. The idea of him having this other side intrigued her.

"Rhiannon was asking about you at LoBar last night," Chad said.

Rhiannon Michaels? Angela wondered. Chad had to be talking about the sleek, sexy siren pursued by half the men in town.

Bryan's flush deepened, and Angela's interest piqued.

When Chad left and they were alone again, Angela decided to indulge her curiosity. "So you know Rhiannon," she said.

"Yeah. We, uh, we dated for a while."

That confirmed it, then. Bryan was definitely more party guy than serious businessman. Rhiannon only dated the wild ones—the men who only dated women like her.

Not that Angela believed she was ugly, but it took a particular kind of man to appreciate her and she was becoming less and less sure that Bryan was that kind of man. She hadn't missed the disappointment on his face at their first meeting yesterday, but later, in the ballroom, she'd felt a definite zing of attraction. Those contradictory reactions had confused her—a feeling exacerbated by his appearance tonight. She didn't like this push-pull sensation because it recalled times she hadn't been so secure in herself. She had a great life without a man complicating things.

Of course, it wasn't men in general she objected to, just ones who might break her heart. Like a good-looking, charming party boy out for a good time, a fling. A fling that was guaranteed not to lead to anything serious—since the very definition of a party guy was that he couldn't *be* serious—was another possibility altogether.

Could she date a guy and not end up with her heart broken? Was she capable of that kind of cavalier, temporary engagement? Maybe with some guys, but with Bryan—she wasn't so sure. She watched him out of the corner of her eye as he laughed at something Tanya said. She hadn't been this attracted to a man since Troy. And frankly, that worried her. A lot.

THE NEXT DAY was Bryan's day off, so he and Zephyr went snowboarding. It felt good to trade his suits and ties for fleece and board pants. Fun didn't have a high priority in his life these days, but it was still a fundamental part of him.

"Where were you last night?" Zephyr asked as they rode the Red Lady Express lift to the top of the mountain. "I looked for you at LoBar."

"I dropped by the Mountain Theatre group for a while."

"You thinking of going on the stage? Becoming an actor? That's radical."

"No. The hotel is hosting a fund-raiser for the group and they invited me to come by and meet people."

"A fund-raiser? What kind?"

"A fancy party with chocolate desserts and a silent auction."

"Chocolate!" Zephyr grinned. "Maybe Trish and I should make an appearance."

"It's a hundred bucks a couple."

Zephyr's smile vanished. "Maybe not, then." He brightened once more. "But hey, you and someone from the theater should come on my show and talk it up."

Bryan knew his boss would like that. Nothing made Carl happier than publicity for the hotel. "All right. I'll ask Angela when she's available."

They glided off the lift and stopped to adjust their bindings. "Who is Angela?" Zephyr asked.

"Angela Krizova. She owns the Chocolate Moose." But apparently making chocolate wasn't her only talent. He still couldn't get over her transformation onstage last night. "She's coordinating the fund-raiser."

"Cool." Zephyr straightened and unzipped his parka partway. "Maybe she can make some chocolate recipes on the show or something."

Bryan laughed. "You want her to cook?"

"Why not? Food sells. So does sex, but you can't do that on TV—at least not on my show."

The thought of Angela and sex sent a jolt through him. There was a definite sensuality about her, something Bryan was aware of every time he was with her. His attraction to her was unsettling. He'd never pictured himself with a woman who probably weighed more than he did, but when he'd been with Angela last night, he hadn't thought about her size—except to notice the soft roundness of her hips or generous curves of her breasts. He shook his head, trying to clear it.

"This weekend I'm broadcasting live coverage of the Al Johnson Memorial Race," Zephyr said.

"Oh, yeah? What are you going to do? Show footage of all the crazy costumes and stuff?"

"That, and I'll interview some of the entrants. But first I put together a short film about Al Johnson." Al had been an early mail carrier in Crested Butte, one who lived up to the old saying about neither rain nor sleet nor gloom of night preventing the mail getting through. Al delivered the mail on skis, over mountain passes, sometimes in blizzard conditions. "I got Hagan to dress up in old-fashioned gear with a big mailbag we borrowed from the museum and I filmed the whole thing in black-and-white," Zephyr said.

"Hagan is probably the only one who could ski on those big, old wooden skis," Bryan said. Hagan Ansdar, a Crested Butte ski patroller originally from Norway, had won the race two years previously, skiing with conventional telemark gear, but dressed in a ratty raccoon coat someone had unearthed from a basement.

"He's working this year, so he said this was as close as he could get to participating," Zephyr said. "Maddie will be there, too, on call as an EMT."

Maddie and Hagan's wedding had been the third one Bryan had attended this past summer—the one that had turned his thoughts toward settling down. If a former playboy and ski bum like Hagan could find happiness with marriage and starting his own computer software company, then why couldn't Bryan make similar big changes in his life?

They headed down the run, bombing through drifts of powder, carving wide turns on the steeps. They let out loud whoops as they raced each other through a stand of trees, then skidded into the lift line, red faced from the cold and grinning ear to ear.

"Magic!" Zephyr said, exchanging high fives with his friend. "I've missed being out here with you, dude."

"This is great," Bryan agreed. They inched their way to the head of the line and flashed their passes for the liftie.

On the chair once more, Zephyr said, "Rhiannon was asking about you last night. That Rachel chick from the hotel said she'd tried to talk you into coming with her, but you turned her down."

"I told you, I had to go to the theater group."

"Trying to score points with the boss, huh?" Zephyr shook his head. "Better you than me. I couldn't handle that corporate BS."

"It's not so bad," Bryan said. "I enjoy the work, most of the time. And this is just a stepping stone. One day I want to open my own hotel. A smaller, boutique place where I can do things the way I want. Right now I'm paying my dues." And he had a lot of dues to pay. At twenty-eight, he had a long way to go to catch up with guys who'd gone straight to work out of college. He didn't want to be an old man before he realized his dream, so he had to work extra hard and move up the ladder quickly.

"I told everybody you hadn't really sold out to the man," Zephyr said. "I told them this was all part of a plan."

"Who thinks I sold out?" Bryan asked.

"Oh, you know." Zephyr waved one hand. "Just some people shooting off their mouths. It doesn't matter."

But it did matter to Bryan. It annoyed him—and yeah, it hurt some, too—that his friends had so little faith in him.

"So, who all did you meet last night?" Zephyr asked. "Anybody interesting? That new director of theirs, Tanya Bledso, is pretty hot."

"How do you know about Tanya?"

"Dude, I know everything that goes on in this town. I'm plugged in, you know. So, did you meet Tanya?"

"She was there."

"And she's really hot, right?"

"She's okay."

Zephyr grabbed Bryan's wrist and made a show of looking at his own watch.

Bryan jerked away. "What are you doing?"

"Checking your pulse. If you think Tanya is just okay, I'm worried those corporate types have turned you into a zombie."

"Just because I'm not panting after every pretty chick I see doesn't mean I'm a zombie."

"Then what does it mean?"

"Maybe it means I want more out of a relationship than the surface stuff. And don't make any smart remarks about corporate brainwashing or anything."

"Why do you think I'd do that?" Zephyr looked offended. "I'd say it's about time you realized there was more to women than good looks and sex. Not that you can't have all that and a connection on a deeper level. Look at me and Trish."

Bryan was glad to shift the focus of the conversation away

from himself. "I'm still trying to figure out what she sees in you," he said.

"Haven't you heard opposites attract? We balance each other out. I help her loosen up and she brings out my intellectual side."

"I didn't know you had an intellectual side."

Zephyr punched Bryan's arm, and Bryan punched him back. Just like old times.

"Seriously, what are you looking for in the perfect woman?" Zephyr asked as they unloaded from the lift again. "Maybe I can help you find her."

Bryan started to make some remark about not needing Zephyr as a matchmaker, but stopped. The truth was, Zephyr *did* know almost everyone in town, and he was a more astute judge of character than people gave him credit for. "I'm looking for a woman who'll take me seriously," he said. "Someone who can see beyond my partying past."

"I dig it. You want a chick who sees you're more than just a pretty face and a good time."

"Something like that." And maybe he wanted a woman who had more going for her than looks alone. Not that he thought beautiful women were shallow. He knew plenty of smart, savvy and sexy chicks. But so far he hadn't made a real connection with any of them.

"I'll have to think on this awhile," Zephyr said. "Somewhere there has got to be the perfect woman for you."

"Thanks, but I'd as soon find her on my own."

"Doesn't mean I can't keep my eyes open to help you out. After all, sometimes our friends know us better than we know ourselves."

If that was true, Bryan thought, then he was in trouble. His friends apparently saw him as either a sellout or a slacker. Neither was a very flattering picture.

Chapter Three

The Al Johnson Memorial Uphill Downhill Race commemorated the exploits of a pioneering mail carrier, but in typical Crested Butte fashion, it featured competitors in zany costumes, a carnival atmosphere and an excuse for locals and visitors alike to party.

While Angela wouldn't be caught dead barreling up a six-hundred-foot incline while dressed in a large, pink bunny costume or similar outlandish garb, she was happy to volunteer her services handing out hot chocolate to race participants and fans at the base of the Silver Queen lift. From there, participants made their way to the starting point at the bottom of the North Face lift. Racers could choose to ski the entire course by themselves, but many opted to form relay teams, with one racer handling the uphill portion, the other the downhill. Keeping with the spirit of commemorating Al Johnson's legacy, the uphill racer had to deliver a letter to his or her team member.

Other than that, anything went, and did. As she dispensed paper cups of cocoa, Angela saw teams dressed as a hot dog and a jar of mustard, Betty and Barney Rubble, twin tigers and Batman and Robin.

"Zephyr looks almost ordinary in this crowd," said Trish Sanders, who was serving coffee next to Angela.

"Is he racing?" Angela asked. Though she'd never personally met the colorful snowboarder and rock guitarist turned talk-show host, Zephyr was the kind of person it was impossible to ignore.

"No, he's filming for his show. Oh, there he is. With Max." Trish pointed to where the blond-dreadlocked boarder was interviewing a burly skier who was dressed in a Colorado Avalanche hockey uniform.

Max Overbridge owned the snowboard and bicycle shop just down from the Chocolate Moose. A second man in a hockey uniform joined him. "Who's that?" Angela asked.

"Eric Sepulveda, a ski patroller," Trish said. "Looks like he and Max have teamed up for the race."

"Can a thirsty volunteer get a drink here?" A petite woman with a short cap of white-blond hair approached the refreshment booths. She was accompanied by a black Labrador retriever who wore a red search-and-rescue vest.

"Casey!" Trish leaned over the table to hug the blonde, then turned to introduce Angela. "You know Casey Overbridge, right? Max's wife?"

"I'm one of her best customers," Casey said. She accepted a cup of hot chocolate from Angela.

"Are you and your dog working today?" Angela asked, nodding at the Lab.

"We're on call," Casey said. "Though I hope we don't have to rescue anyone. Mainly Lucy and I are here as publicity for Search and Rescue." She patted the black Lab, who grinned up at her and wagged her tail.

Casey straightened and looked past Angela. "Bryan!" she called and waved.

"Hey, Casey."

Angela's stomach fluttered at the sound of the familiar low voice behind her. Then Bryan was standing beside her, handsome in a blue-and-gray sweater over gray pants and black boots. She smoothed the fake-fur collar of her parka, glad she'd decided on the curve-hugging wool skirt instead of jeans.

"Hello, Angela," he said, his eyes meeting hers.

"Hi, Bryan."

"You aren't racing?" Casey asked.

Bryan shook his head. "The hotel's hosting the awards ceremony," he said. "I'm coordinating that."

"How do you like your new job?" Casey asked.

"It's good."

"Do people always dress so strangely for this?" An older man joined them. He, too, wore a sweater over gray pants. A name tag identified him as Carl Phelps, manager of the Elevation Hotel. He stared as a large carton of French fries and a bottle of ketchup skied past.

"This is pretty normal for any kind of Crested Butte celebration," Bryan said.

"They certainly don't have anything like this in Michigan," Carl said, as a man in a flowered housedress over long underwear accepted a cup of coffee from Trish.

"They don't have anything like this anywhere else," Bryan said. "It's one of the things that makes Crested Butte special."

"Or at least different," Carl conceded. He turned to Bryan. "Is everything ready for the awards ceremony?"

"It's all set," Bryan said.

"I'll be filming the whole thing for my show." Zephyr joined them and held up his video camera. "A hundred percent digital and state of the art."

"Sweet." Bryan examined the camera. "Where did you get this?"

"Trish gave it to me for Christmas." Zephyr grinned at his girlfriend, who beamed back. "It pays to hook up with the right woman."

"Aw, that's so sweet," Casey said.

"Too sweet for me," Angela said. "And I'm a woman who loves sugar."

"Everything seems to be running smoothly here," Carl said. He clapped a hand on Bryan's shoulder. "You and I have business to attend to inside."

Bryan's expression clouded, but he quickly assumed an all-business attitude. "Of course." He nodded to the group. "I'll see you all at the awards ceremony."

"We wouldn't miss it," Casey said.

"I'd better get busy, too." Zephyr shouldered the camera once more. "I'm going to film the uphill and downhill segments of the race."

"I can't get used to seeing Bryan with his nose to the grindstone," Trish said. "Any other year, he'd be out there with Zephyr, clowning around with the racers."

"Some of us do have to work for a living," Angela said. For some reason she felt the need to defend Bryan. There were worse things than a guy hanging up his beer steins for gainful employment.

"Yes, everyone has to grow up sometime." Trish laughed. "Except, of course, Zephyr."

Angela studied her friend as Trish turned to serve coffee to a couple of tourists. Like Angela, Trish had her own successful business. She was known around town as a smart woman who had everything going for her. People were still scratching their heads over her relationship with the lovable but extremely laid-back Zephyr. Angela figured it had to be true love. Why else would two such different people be drawn together?

"Angela, tell me more about this theater fund-raiser," Casey said. "I saw some flyers around town."

"The money will go to license new scripts and pay for new scenery and costumes," Angela said. "And we'd like to offer a summer program for children."

"Will you be supplying the chocolate?" Casey asked.

"Of course."

"Then I am so there," Casey said.

"Bryan's helping you put this together, isn't he?" Trish asked, rejoining the conversation.

"Yes. He's the liaison at the hotel."

Trish nodded. "Zephyr mentioned it. Apparently, he's decided he needs to fix Bryan up with someone. He was asking me last night if I knew any single women who would be a good match for him."

"As if Bryan needs help meeting women," Casey said. "He's good-looking, fun to be with, smart. I've seen him around with plenty of cute girls."

"He never has any problem finding dates," Trish said. "I'm really not sure what Zephyr was getting at. There are a lot of women around town who'd love to have a nice guy like Bryan—especially now that he has a good job."

"Employment is a plus," Casey agreed. She looked around them. "I'm guessing the race has started. I think I'll get my skis, and Lucy and I will head over toward the finish line."

"See you at the awards ceremony," Trish said.

"Guess we can pack up here," Angela said. She drained the last of the hot chocolate into a cup and began disconnecting the pot to haul back to her store. The discussion of

Bryan's need for a girlfriend—and the plethora of women he had to choose from—had disturbed her. Did anyone think of *her* as a likely companion for the handsome hotel manager? Or would they laugh if she suggested it?

She'd parked on the other side of the building, so the shortest route to her car was through the hotel. She was passing a row of offices when Bryan appeared in a doorway. "Angela, can I talk to you a minute?" he asked.

"Sure." She shifted the chocolate pot and a carton of cups to one hip. "What can I do for you?"

"Let me take those." He relieved her of her burden. "Come in here." He ushered her into the office. "Sit down," he said, gesturing to a pair of upholstered chairs.

She sat and he deposited the pot and cups on a credenza and took the chair beside her. "Do you have everything you need for the fund-raiser?" he asked.

"Yes. Marco and I settled on a menu, and the publicity committee has flyers plastered all over town. I understand ticket sales have been good."

"Good. Would you be interested in a little more publicity?"

"There's no such thing as too much." She gave him her warmest smile. "What did you have in mind?"

"Zephyr's asked us to appear on his show to talk about the fund-raiser."

"The two of us? Together?" She took a deep breath, trying to quell the nervous fluttering in her chest. She reminded herself Bryan was asking her to help him with a business issue, not for a date.

"Or you could go on the show by yourself, or with someone else from the theater. I realize I'm not really a part of that—"

"No, we should do it together," she said. "You can talk

about the hotel, and I'll talk about the theater." And she'd get to spend a little more time with him.

"And chocolate. Zephyr suggested you cook something."

"Free publicity for my business, too? I can't wait."

"Great." He looked relieved. "Some people think Zephyr is kind of a flake, but under that goofy exterior is a really smart guy. I think his show is turning into a success."

"I learned a long time ago that you can never judge a person by outward appearances," she said. "I've met shy, milquetoast types who turned out to be fiery actors and blowhards who couldn't deliver a convincing line to save their lives."

"I've never had a desire to act, but I'll admit that what I saw the other night was interesting," Bryan said. "And you're really talented."

"Thank you." She would never get tired of hearing his praise or of seeing that appreciative look in his eyes. "When does Zephyr want to do this show?"

"I'll have to talk to him and get back to you. Soon, since the fund-raiser's only two weeks away."

"Great." She could sit here all afternoon making small talk with him, but they both had work to do. Besides, one lesson she'd learned in the theater that had served her well in real life was to always leave them wanting more. "I'll talk to you soon," she said, standing.

He rose also. "Soon," he said, his eyes locked to hers.

She started to gather up her boxes, but he stopped her. "I'll get these for you," he said.

"Thank you. I hate to keep you from your work."

He made a face. "It's nothing that won't wait." He leaned close, his voice low. "To tell you the truth, about a third of what I do is either busywork or corporate BS. A lot of paperwork."

"I suppose every job has boring aspects like that," she said. "Even working for myself I have to do taxes and stuff."

"It's a trade-off, I guess," he said as they walked to her car. "We do what we have to in order to get what we want."

And what do you want, Bryan? It was a loaded question, one she didn't feel she knew him well enough to ask. Besides, if rumors were correct, there would be a picket fence in his future. And given his initial reaction to her—even though he'd warmed considerably since then—she suspected she didn't fill that role any more than the other leading roles she left to others.

ON A FROSTY but sunny morning in early March, Angela, Bryan, Zephyr and Zephyr's cameraman—a silent, freckle-faced young guy named Brix—met at the Chocolate Moose to shoot footage for *The Z Hour.* It was Bryan's first visit to the shop, though he'd passed it hundreds of times on his way to Max's snowboard store.

The rich aromas of chocolate and vanilla greeted him as soon as he entered the large front room. A handful of small tables and chairs were arranged in front of a long, glass display case filled with cakes, cookies and candies. Twin coffee and cocoa urns flanked the cash register, and a large moose head, adorned with sunglasses and a lei, looked out over the scene.

"You and Zephyr can put these on," Angela said. She handed them each aprons.

Bryan unfolded his and studied a cartoon of a grinning moose. "The best things in life are chocolate," he read.

"I don't know about that," Zephyr said, tying on his apron. "What about rock and roll? Or sex? Or beer?"

"In my shop, the best thing in life is chocolate," she asserted.

Bryan could have argued with that. He liked chocolate well enough, but found the woman before him much more interesting than her candies. Beneath her own apron she wore a red turtleneck sweater, dark jeans and black leather boots with tall heels—clothes that emphasized her curves and height.

"Do you have one of those hat things, too?" Zephyr asked. "A toucan or whatever it's called?"

"A toque. Here you go." She handed the two men tall, paper chef's hats, then donned her own headgear.

"Sweet!" Zephyr admired himself in the mirror, then turned to Brix and gave him a thumbs up. "Let's get this show on the road."

While Brix and Zephyr conferred, Bryan sidled over to Angela. He leaned in close enough to smell her vanilla-and-spice perfume. "Do I have this hat on right?" he asked.

"You look great." Pitched slightly above a whisper, her sultry voice sent heat straight through him.

"Quiet on the set!" Zephyr bellowed, loud enough to make Angela jump. The manic blond grabbed an electric guitar, played a loud fanfare, then grinned at the camera. "Welcome to *The Z Hour.* I'm Zephyr and every week I bring you the hippest and hottest happenings of Crested Butte and beyond. Today we're at the Chocolate Moose, visiting with the owner, Angela Krizova. Also joining us is Bryan Perry of the Elevation Hotel at Crested Butte Mountain Resort. The two of them are going to show us how to make chocolate truffles and talk about the fund-raiser they're coordinating at the Elevation Hotel to benefit the Mountain Theatre community theater group here in C.B. Take it away, Angela."

He swung around and pointed the neck of the guitar at her. Though Bryan's stomach was doing backflips at the thought of appearing on camera, Angela was as serene as if she did this every day of the week. Obviously her acting experience helped. She smiled for the camera and said, "Thanks, Zephyr. Today, I'm going to show you how I make my sinfully delicious dark chocolate truffles."

"What makes them so sinful?" Zephyr asked.

"The chocolate is so rich and sweet and sensuous—" she lowered her voice to an intimate tease "—one bite and I think you'll agree that anything so good has to be a little bit *naughty*."

"What do you think about that, Bryan?" Zephyr asked.

Bryan sucked in a deep breath and tried to look calm. Focusing on Angela instead of the camera helped. "I think Angela wants to lead us astray," he said.

She smirked. "You men are so easily led." She moved a bowl to the center of the counter and uncovered it. "Come over here and I'll show you what to do. First, wash your hands."

They dutifully washed and dried their hands, then arranged themselves on either side of her at the counter. "This bowl contains chocolate ganache," she explained, scooping out several clumps of glossy, dark goo. "It's made with cream and chocolate shavings. I've refrigerated it so it's thick enough to be shaped. So start by pinching up a little ganache and rolling it into a ball in your palms."

She demonstrated, and Zephyr and Bryan attempted to copy her. Angela made it look easy, but the ganache immediately stuck to Bryan's hands and refused to form any kind of sphere.

Angela had six little balls lined up on the counter in front of her by the time she noticed the two men had made no progress at all. "Having problems?" she asked.

"It's tougher than it looks," Bryan said. He frowned at the gloppy mass of chocolate in his hand.

"It's sticky," Zephyr said. He licked chocolate off his fingers. "But it tastes good."

"You're being too rough," she scolded. She scooped up a fresh bit of ganache and demonstrated the technique again. "You want to roll it lightly and work quickly. Think of the chocolate as being like a woman."

The men exchanged glances. "How is chocolate like a woman?" Zephyr asked. "Is this a new joke?"

"No, it's not a joke." She shaped another sphere. "This chocolate is like a woman because with the right gentle touch it becomes pliable and smooth. But apply too much pressure or allow too much heat to build up and it won't cooperate at all."

"So the secret is knowing how to touch it," Bryan asked. No woman had ever complained about his skills as a lover before, but that didn't mean he couldn't learn something new. He copied Angela's movements once more, getting it right this time.

"That's good." She leaned closer to examine his efforts. "Coax it into the right shape."

Zephyr had abandoned trying to shape the chocolate into spheres and was busy making a pile of irregular pellets. "What are you doing?" Bryan asked.

"Moose droppings," Zephyr said, and popped one into his mouth.

Angela slapped his hand away. "Maybe you'd better just watch." She set the bowl of ganache aside and reached for a second bowl in which sat a flour sifter. "Next, we'll cover the balls with powdered cocoa. This helps to set the shape." She cranked the handle of the sifter and a cloud of cocoa drifted over the ganache.

"You finish them," she said, and handed the sifter to Bryan. While he cranked, she turned the balls over until they were coated on all sides.

"Now what?" Zephyr asked. "Is it time to eat them?"

"No." She slapped his hand away once more. "Now we coat them in a chocolate glaze." She retrieved two more bowls from the counter behind her. "I have a white chocolate glaze and a dark chocolate glaze. Simply dip a truffle in the glaze, set it aside to dry, and you're done."

"That looks really messy," Bryan said as he watched her dip the chocolates by hand.

"It is. That's half the fun. It's about experiencing the chocolate fully—sensually, from its creation to the last luscious, melting bite."

After this show aired, she'd probably have a line out the door of men who would happily pay for the privilege of hearing her describe the sensual nature of chocolate in her throaty, alluring voice.

Bryan picked up a truffle and plunged it into the bowl of white chocolate. It immediately slipped out of his hand. He stifled a curse.

"What's wrong?" Angela asked.

"I dropped it."

"That happens sometimes," she said. "Just fish it out."

He probed the bowl of chocolate, sloshing some over the side, but the truffle eluded capture. "It's a slippery little devil," he said.

"Let me help." Angela plunged her hand in alongside his, her fingers brushing against his in the slightly warm, silken chocolate. A disconcerting image of naked bodies smeared with chocolate flashed through Bryan's mind. He couldn't resist purposely stroking the back of her hand. "I see what you mean about this being a sensuous experience," he said.

She jerked her hand from the bowl. "We'll find it later," she said, avoiding looking at him. "For now, let's use the dark chocolate."

While she washed her hands, he managed to dip and retrieve the rest of the truffles and set them to dry on a wire rack on the counter.

"Now can we eat them?" Zephyr asked.

"They need to set up first," Angela said. "While we wait, let's talk about the Mountain Theatre fund-raiser."

The fund-raiser. Right. The reason they were here.

The two men washed their hands and joined Angela at one of the little tables. Zephyr once more assumed the role of television host. "Tell us all about this fund-raiser," he said.

Bryan and Angela had talked on the phone the previous evening and discussed what they should say. "The event is being held at the Elevation Hotel this coming Saturday, beginning at 7:00 p.m.," Angela began.

"It's a chocolate extravaganza," Bryan added. "Angela will be making some special chocolate desserts."

"Yes, I'm working on some recipes especially for it."

"Tickets can be purchased at the hotel or from any Mountain Theatre member," Bryan said.

"And here at the Chocolate Moose," Angela added. "All the proceeds go to support the Crested Butte Mountain Theatre, which has been active in the community for over thirty-five years."

"Now can we eat the chocolate?" Zephyr asked.

"Yes. It's all yours."

She selected a truffle and bit into it. Mesmerized, Bryan watched her tongue flick out to capture a stray bit of chocolate on her lip. He looked away, for fear of embarrassing himself. You'd think he'd never seen a woman eat before!

"Primo chocolate!" Zephyr declared. He grabbed his guitar and began strumming a tune. "Don't trifle with the truffles that Angela makes. Treat yourself to all the goodies that Angela bakes. Support our local actors, for heaven's sake! Get your tickets to the party—you know it will be great!"

The last chords of this chorus still rang in Bryan's ears when Zephyr pronounced they were done, and Angela began clearing away the bowls and remaining truffles. "Do you want to take these back to the hotel for your coworkers?" she asked. "I can box them up for you."

"Thanks. That would be great." He picked up the bowls of glaze and followed her into a back room that contained two refrigerators, a freezer and four sets of steel shelving filled with bags of sugar, flour and cocoa, boxes of chocolate chips, egg white powder and other ingredients he couldn't identify.

"You can put those bowls in the first refrigerator." She nodded toward a white side-by-side model, then pulled a flattened box off the top of one of the shelving units. With a practiced move, she popped it open and began arranging the truffles inside.

Bryan leaned against the refrigerator, arms crossed. "This was fun today," he said. "I enjoyed seeing what you do."

"I love my work," she said. "And I guess it shows." She laughed. "In more ways than one. But I always say, never trust a skinny cook."

"You look great," he said. He couldn't believe he'd never noticed her before; now that he knew her, he couldn't keep his eyes off her.

Her cheeks turned pink. "Thanks." She moved past him, into the front room once more.

"We should go out sometime," he said.

She juggled the box of truffles, then carefully set it on the counter and turned to face him. "Go out?"

"Yeah, you know. On a date."

For the first time that day, she looked flustered, but she quickly recovered. "Sure. That would be fun. What do you want to do? Catch a band at LoBar or go for pizza at the Last Steep?"

Those were the kind of dates he had in his slacker days. Now he wanted to do something classier, more grown-up. "I was thinking I'd take you to dinner at Garlic Mike's." The intimate Italian eatery on the outskirts of Gunnison had been voted Most Romantic Restaurant in a local newspaper poll.

Angela's eyes widened. "Oh. Well. I don't know—"

"How about Friday night?"

She shook her head. "I have too much to do to get ready for the fund-raiser on Saturday."

"Then you choose a night."

She turned and began rearranging a display of Chocolate Moose coffee mugs on a nearby shelf. "Maybe now isn't a good time. I have the play and rehearsals and a lot of work getting ready for the fund-raiser."

Was she *rejecting* him? Deep breath. Time to regroup. He couldn't remember when a woman had turned him down. In fact, he was pretty sure this was a first.

He looked around the shop, searching for inspiration. He found it in a poster advertising the upcoming performances of *I Hate Hamlet.* "What about Sunday night?" he said. "The fund-raiser will be over and the play doesn't start until the next week."

She shook her head. "No. I'd better not."

He stood very still, working hard to keep his feelings from

showing in his face. She really was turning him down. And why? The two of them got along great. "Is there something in particular about me you don't like?" he asked stiffly.

"No!" She whirled to face him, her eyes wide with surprise, her cheeks flushed. "I like you. I really do."

He believed her. She was a good actress, but he didn't think she was faking it now. And he hadn't imagined the heat between them when their hands had brushed in the bowl of chocolate. "Are you dating someone else?" he asked. That had to be the answer. She probably had some big bruiser of a boy-friend who'd like nothing better than to pound any potential rival.

"No." She turned away and began wiping down the hot chocolate machine. "I just…I have too much else going on right now to start dating anyone," she said. "It's so hard juggling everything. I have to be at the theater practically every night, and the shop takes up all my time during the days. I guess that's life in a tourist town during the busy season."

There was more to her reluctance to go out with him than a lack of time, he was sure. "Maybe later, then," he said, doing his best to sound unaffected by her rejection, though inside he was crushed. And confused—both by her reluctance and by his own attraction to a woman who was nothing like any other woman he'd wanted to spend time with. He was a guy who always dated the hottest girl in any crowd. Angela wasn't that kind of girl—though for some reason she certainly raised *his* temperature. He couldn't figure it out, but he wanted her to at least give him a chance to try.

She flashed one of her dazzling smiles. "Maybe. Thanks for being understanding."

That was him. Mr. Understanding. Not. "I'd better get back to the hotel," he said.

She nodded. "Thanks. I'll see you Saturday."

"Saturday?"

"At the fund-raiser. Or will you be there?"

"I'll be there." He rushed out the door before she could say more, into a world of swirling snow. A spring storm was bringing fresh powder to the slopes and a clean, white topping to the dirty piles of snow lining the streets. He thought of the white chocolate glaze Angela had used for the truffles and the sensuous feel of their fingers entwined in the chocolate. He couldn't say he'd ever experienced anything like that with any other woman.

He straightened his shoulders and strode down the street. Angela had turned him down once, but he wasn't the kind of man who gave up that easily. He hadn't let others' criticism keep him from pursuing his dreams, and he wouldn't let Angela's reluctance stop him from pursuing her. For his own peace of mind, he needed to figure out what it was about Angela that drew him to her. If she wanted to play hard to get, she'd find out he wasn't a man who liked to take no for an answer.

Chapter Four

Bryan wasn't the type to suffer from nerves, but the night of the theater fund-raiser, he had to struggle to keep from constantly fidgeting with his tie and smoothing his hair. He wanted everything to go smoothly to prove to Mr. Phelps that he was capable of handling more responsibility. Some of Bryan's friends would be attending this event also. He wanted them to see him as competent and successful in his new role.

So far, so good. Everything was in place, the tables draped in white cloths, each with a centerpiece of glittering comedy and tragedy masks. The tables for refreshments and silent-auction items were set up, the DJ had everything he needed to provide music for dancing, and the PA system was working. There was even a coat check for the guests. The gift certificate with the hotel's own contribution—a weekend's stay—was already in the hands of the woman who was in charge of the silent auction.

Judging from the turnout, the fund-raiser was going to be a big success. He searched for Angela, but couldn't find her. Maybe she was already on the dance floor, in the arms of some theater type. His stomach clenched tighter at the thought. Why had he ever assumed a woman like Angela would be unattached? She was sexy, fun and successful; she probably had all kinds of men trailing after her.

"Everything all right?"

Bryan suppressed a grimace and turned to greet his boss. "Carl. I didn't expect to see you here."

The manager tugged at the collar of his dark suit. "My wife and I decided we should make an appearance, try to be more involved with the community." He looked out over the ballroom. "I'm here if you need anything."

"I have it all under control."

"You made sure the theater group understands the occupancy limits of the fire code?" Phelps asked.

"We discussed all that when the contract was signed," Bryan said. "They agreed to limit ticket sales."

"And they understood they are not to park in the section of the garage reserved for hotel guests?"

"I explained we had ample parking for visitors near the garage elevators."

"And about the catering—"

"Everything is under control," Bryan said again. Why was Carl giving him such a hard time? Didn't the man trust him?

Obviously, no. Bryan clenched his jaw. *Welcome to the world of middle management,* he thought. Nothing he hadn't expected, and something he had to put up with in order to realize his dreams. That didn't stop the scrutiny from irritating him, however.

"Good. That's good to hear." Carl waited, as if expecting Bryan to say more. But Bryan had already learned that the less said, the less Carl could find to object to.

Bryan spotted Angela over by the refreshment table. "I'd better speak with Ms. Krizova," he said. Without waiting for a reply, he started across the room.

Glad of the chance to talk with Angela, he approached the table where she was arranging trays of truffles. "Hello, Angela," he said. "You look great."

She looked up, her smile radiant. "Thank you, Bryan." Her dark hair was gathered into a loose chignon at the nape of her neck, drawing attention to the fine bones of her face and the long column of her neck. The low neckline of her wine-red velvet dress revealed a distracting hint of cleavage. Bryan forced himself to keep his gaze on her eyes, which were definitely worth looking at, their green depths accented by artful makeup.

"Is there something you needed?" she asked.

He realized he'd been staring—again—and forced his gaze away. "I wanted to make sure you had everything you needed," he said.

"Yes. Everything looks wonderful." She looked around the room, at the women in sparkling dresses and pantsuits, the men in less vibrant but just as formal suits. They milled around the food or swayed on the dance floor to classic rock and pop tunes. "I think all the guests are having a good time," she said.

"What about you?" he asked. "Are you getting a chance to enjoy yourself?"

"Of course. It's always fun seeing friends. And everyone's raving about my chocolates." She leaned forward to fill in an empty spot on one of the trays.

"These truffles are to die for!" Casey, wearing an electric blue minidress with silver spangles, selected a white chocolate truffle from a tray and bit into it.

"Thanks," Angela said. "I love your dress."

Casey shrugged. "My mom was only too happy to send it to me when I told her I needed something for a fancy social event. I told her to pull something from my closet back home. I figured this was a chance to get more use out of the stuff I wore to all those charity dinners and political fund-raisers in Chicago." Casey, who worked for the local Chamber of Commerce, fit into Crested Butte's laid-back scene so well that Bryan had forgotten that before moving to town she had been a reluctant socialite in the Windy City.

"The trick was coordinating my outfit with hers." Max appeared behind his wife, stroking an electric blue bow tie with silver spangles. It stood out against his starched white shirt and plain dark suit. "Did you know you can buy anything on the Internet?"

"Don't let Zephyr see that tie or he'll want one," Bryan said.

"I already promised to give it to him when I'm done," Max said.

"I saw you two on Zephyr's show earlier this week," Casey said. "You looked like you were having a good time."

"Yeah, it was a lot of fun," Bryan said, watching Angela's face to gauge her assessment.

"It was," Angela agreed. "Though I don't think I have to worry about losing my candy-making gig to Zephyr or Bryan."

"Hey, everybody here at work said the truffles I made were great," Bryan said.

"People at work will eat anything," Max said. "Leftover Halloween candy, stale pretzels—you name it. If it shows up in the employee break room and it's free, it'll get eaten."

"Stale pretzels and Angela's awesome truffles don't even belong in the same sentence." Casey selected another candy from the tray. "Even if Bryan helped put them together, I know the chocolate was all Angela and she's the expert."

"This next set of songs is for everyone who's requested I slow things down a little," the DJ announced. "So cuddle up, all you lovebirds."

"Can I tear you away from the chocolate long enough to dance?" Max asked his wife.

"I could be persuaded." She gave him a coy look, then slipped her hand into his and allowed him to lead her onto the dance floor.

Bryan turned to Angela. "Would you like to dance?"

"I should probably stay and watch the chocolates," she said.

"You don't strike me as a woman who wants to spend all evening behind a table watching over sweets," he said. "Don't you get enough of that at work?"

He read the hesitation in her expression. "Come on," he urged. "Just one dance. I promise I won't bite."

She laughed. "All right. One dance."

ANGELA ALLOWED BRYAN to take her hand and lead her to the dance floor. While time didn't actually stop or a hush fall over the crowd, a few heads did turn in their direction, and she knew that by Monday morning word would be out that the two of them had been seen dancing close.

Very close. His hand rested comfortably at the small of her back, allowing no room for space between them. The front of his suit coat brushed against her breasts, and even with all the layers of clothing between them, it felt intimate.

Right—somehow.

"I can't believe you've lived here three years and the two of us never met before," he said, gold flecks glinting in his brown eyes as his gaze met hers.

"I guess we just travel in different circles," she said. "I haven't spent much time in clubs or at parties. And I don't snowboard." Did that sound dull to him? Maybe she *was* dull, though she preferred to think of it as settled.

"Still, you'd think we would have run into each other before now," he said.

"Maybe we did and you didn't notice me." It wouldn't be the first time a man had looked right past her, to focus on a prettier—and yes, *thinner*—woman.

"No, I would have remembered you." He emphasized the words with a squeeze and an intense look that sent a tingling sensation clear to her toes.

She'd have remembered him, too. He was exactly the kind of man she always noticed—with dark hair and eyes, an expressive face and an outgoing personality.

Leading man material, she'd dubbed the type, long before she met Troy and was caught up in his spell.

"How are rehearsals going?" he asked.

"Typical chaos two weeks before we open," she said, glad to move the conversation to what felt like less emotionally dangerous territory. "Nobody can remember their lines, some of the costumes and sets aren't finished, and we're all sure we have a disaster on our hands."

"How are you going to open on time?"

"It will all come together. It always does. It's part of the magic of theater. There are even people who believe that the worse things are right before the opening, the better the show will be."

"Do you believe that?"

She considered the question a moment. "There's something to be said for getting all the disasters out of the way before a paying audience shows up," she said.

"I wonder if that would work in other areas of life?" he mused.

"What do you mean?"

"Say you had a big job interview. The week before, you could have a rehearsal interview. You'd get all the foot-in-mouth verbal mistakes, spilled coffee and mismatched socks out of the way ahead of the real thing."

"That might work," she said, smiling. "Maybe you should start a new business offering that service."

"Or how about a rehearsal date?" he continued. "Get all the bad hair and disastrous conversational tangents and awkward silences out of your system and guarantee a good time on the real date."

She laughed. "Have you really had dates that were that bad?" she asked.

"A few." The music ended and they pulled apart. She sensed he was as reluctant to leave her as she was to move away from him. "Mostly they were my fault. Usually when I tried to date women who were too classy for me."

She let her gaze linger on his broad shoulders, neatly trimmed hair and tailored suit. "I can't picture any woman being too classy for you," she said.

"You should have seen me a few years ago."

A few years ago, she'd been an emotional wreck, her heart and her self-esteem trampled. It had taken a long time to put herself back together. A few weeks ago, she would have said she was doing great; nothing could faze her. One smile from Bryan, one brush from his hand, and she'd realized how weak she still was. She doubted she was strong enough to face all the possibilities—even the bad ones—of pursuing her attraction to him.

They returned to the refreshment table and lingered around the punch bowl, the conversation momentarily stalled, but neither eager to move away. Angela wanted to ask him more about his time in Crested Butte before she'd known him, but feared this would only lead to questions she didn't care to answer about her own past.

"Bryan! I've been looking all over for you."

They both turned toward the voice, which belonged to a leggy blonde in skintight leather pants and a fur-collared sweater that hugged her large breasts, tiny waist and slim hips. Ignoring Angela, the blonde put a hand on Bryan's arm and leaned close. "Dance with me," she said. "Then I'll let you buy me a drink at the bar and you can tell me where you've been hiding."

Bryan frowned and glanced at Angela, who pretended interest in the punch. "Rhiannon, do you know Angela Krizova?" he asked.

So this was the infamous Rhiannon. Angela had heard all about her from others, but had never had the opportunity to meet the woman who had reportedly once been asked to pose for an issue of *Playboy* dubbed Best of the West.

Rhiannon's gaze swept over Angela in a quick assessment. Angela could almost see the other woman weighing her on an imaginary scale. "We haven't met," Rhiannon said. "Are you the caterer?"

"Speaking of caterers, I'd better make sure Marco took care of the coffee service," Angela said. She nodded in Rhiannon's direction. "It was nice meeting you." Then she hurried away.

Better to have Bryan think she was a flake than stand there and give him more time to compare her to Ms. Leather Pants. Even the strongest woman couldn't bear up long under that kind of scrutiny.

"Whoa! Where are you off to in such a hurry?" Tanya caught Angela by the arm as Angela hurried past.

"I, um, wanted to make sure we weren't running out of truffles," Angela said. She smiled brightly. "Are you having fun? We had a great turnout, didn't we?"

"Yeah, it's great." Tanya leaned closer and scrutinized Angela's face. "Are you okay? You look a little pale."

"I got too hot." She fanned herself. "I'll be fine when I've rested a moment."

"Speaking of hot...I saw you dancing with Bryan." Tanya's smile invited confidences. "You two have really hit it off, haven't you?"

"We're just friends."

"Uh-huh. Isn't that what everyone says when they're trying to cover up the truth about a relationship? As if anyone believes that."

"There is no relationship between me and Bryan Perry, and that's the truth."

"But there's potential there. I recognized that the moment I saw you two looking at each other. There were definite sparks."

"There were?"

"Trust me." Tanya leaned closer and lowered her voice. "So, what are you going to do about him?"

Angela swallowed. While she'd enjoyed fantasizing about her attraction to Bryan, dating him felt like too big a risk. She hated the way her self-confidence deserted her whenever he was around.

"Hey, Angela, Tanya." Casey joined them, her face slightly flushed from dancing. Or maybe from the glass of champagne in her hand. "This is a terrific party," she said. "The Mountain Theatre should do this every year."

"Maybe we will," Tanya said. "That's a great dress."

"Thanks." Casey turned to Angela, eyes shining. "So, what's up with you and Bryan?"

"Nothing is *up* with us. We're just friends."

Casey and Tanya exchanged knowing looks. "He doesn't have a steady girlfriend," Casey said. "And Trish says he told Zephyr he's ready to find Ms. Right and settle down."

The words made Angela's stomach do backflips. "Maybe *I* don't want to settle down," she said, trying to sound as if she meant it. Truthfully, she wasn't opposed to love and marriage and happily ever after, but she was definitely against opening herself up to big-time hurt in the pursuit of a remote possibility.

Her two friends looked smug again, but said nothing. Like Angela, they turned to watch the dance floor. "I see Rhiannon's got her claws out for Bryan again tonight," Casey observed.

"Mmmm," Tanya said. "I thought she was dating Jack Crenshaw."

"They went out one time," Casey said. "Jack is so not her type."

"And Bryan is her type?" Tanya asked.

Casey shook her head. "They had some fun together for a while, I guess, but Zephyr told Trish, who told me, that they broke up because he thought she was too dumb and shallow." She cut her gaze over to Angela. "Bryan isn't into dumb or shallow."

"So he's looking for someone smart," Tanya said. "Someone interested in something besides fashion and gossip. Maybe someone with her own business and interesting hobbies."

"Exactly." Casey finished her champagne. "I've always thought acting was a very interesting hobby."

"Cut it out, you two," Angela said. "Why are you so concerned about this anyway?"

"Think of us as the meddling sisters you never had," Tanya said.

"Yeah," Casey agreed. "You're part of the Crested Butte family now, which gives us carte blanche to insert ourselves in all of your affairs—but only because we love you."

"I appreciate your concern," Angela said. "I think. But why don't you leave it up to Bryan to decide who he's interested in—and who he isn't?"

Casey looked exasperated. "Oh, please! If I'd left it up to Max to decide what he really felt about me, we'd both still be single."

"Don't look at me," Tanya said. "I've already proved I don't know a thing about men."

"All I'm saying is, if you're interested, you should let him know." Casey nudged Angela. "You're definitely a cut above the women he usually dates, so he might be a little intimidated."

Angela was glad she wasn't drinking, or she might have embarrassed herself by shooting wine out of her nose. "Since when is a man who looks like that intimidated by any woman?"

"Come on," Casey said. "All men are still little boys somewhere inside. They get intimidated."

"How do you know this?" Angela asked.

"Yeah," Tanya said. "How do you know?"

Casey glanced around them, then leaned close. "I have to swear you to secrecy first."

"We swear," Tanya said.

Angela nodded.

Casey put up one hand to shield her mouth from view of any potential lip-readers on the dance floor. "Max told me. He swears it's true. All men are intimidated by women at one time or another."

Angela's gaze met Tanya's. This was interesting information, though she wasn't yet sure what it meant.

The song ended and Rhiannon and Bryan moved apart. Someone hailed him from across the room, and he turned in that direction and was soon lost from view. Angela felt a pain around her heart. He was such a great guy, and there was definitely chemistry between the two of them. But chemistry alone didn't guarantee a good outcome. Every cook knew it took the right combination of ingredients *and* the right conditions to create a masterpiece. Get one thing wrong and chocolate mousse became a chocolate mess.

BRYAN WENT INTO WORK Monday fired up for the week. The Mountain Theatre fund-raiser had been the first major event he'd organized on his own and it had gone off without a hitch. Some of the organizers were already talking about returning to the hotel for a similar event next year. At this rate, the raise and greater responsibilities he craved would be his in no time at all. And maybe he could finally convince Zephyr and his other doubting friends that he was serious about making a name for himself in his new career.

Not only had the fund-raiser gone well, but the evening had given him a chance to get to know Angela a little better. He'd enjoyed dancing with her and wished they could have spent more time talking, but other people kept pulling him away. Still, the conversation they had gave him hope that he could persuade her to reconsider her refusal to go out with him. Perhaps because of his past—or because of something in her own history—she was reluctant to move beyond the tentative friendship they'd established. But he was willing to work as hard to change her mind as he was to meet his goals in business.

When Rachel notified him at about ten o'clock that Carl wanted to see him, Bryan went to Carl's office with a smile on his face, sure his boss was going to congratulate him for a job well done.

But Carl didn't return Bryan's smile. He looked downright grim as he motioned for Bryan to take a seat. "I wanted to talk to you about the fund-raiser Saturday night," Carl said.

"I thought it went very well," Bryan said. "Everyone seemed very pleased and there were no problems at all."

"Yes. I heard quite a few people raving about the chocolate truffles that were offered for dessert."

That was what Carl remembered about the evening— Angela's truffles? "Did you try one?" Bryan asked. "They were delicious."

"I checked and Marco confirmed that truffles are not part of our catering menu."

Bryan's stomach knotted. "No. Angela Krizova brought them from her shop, the Chocolate Moose."

The creases on Carl's forehead deepened. "Company policy prohibits any kind of outside food at our catered functions."

"Yes, sir, but I thought an exception should be made in this case, since Ms. Krizova supplying the desserts was something the Mountain Theatre required before they would sign the contract."

"I'm sure if you'd explained the policy to them correctly they would have understood and agreed to comply with our rules."

"What difference does it make whether they bring the dessert or not?" Bryan asked, trying to curb his annoyance. "We catered the rest of the meal."

"With one hundred and sixty people in attendance, one hundred and sixty desserts at seven dollars each—" Carl jabbed at the ten-key calculator on the corner of his desk "—that comes to one thousand, one hundred and twenty dollars in lost revenue. A significant loss."

"Not compared to losing the event altogether."

"I think the chances they'd withdraw on the basis of a few truffles highly unlikely."

"Then why are you so upset? Isn't it our job to keep the customer happy?"

Carl blew out a long breath. "Our job is to keep the customer *and* the stockholders happy," he said. "You don't do that by ignoring over a thousand dollars. I'm sure we have desserts on our catering menu that would have pleased the theater group every bit as well as Ms. Krizova's truffles—though I will agree they were delicious."

"So you did eat one."

"I ate two. Before I realized they had not come from our kitchens."

"I'll keep the policy in mind next time," Bryan said. It was the closest he could bring himself to an apology. As far as he was concerned, he'd done nothing wrong.

"A man does not get ahead in this business by ignoring rules," Carl said sternly.

Bryan started to argue that stupid rules deserved to be ignored, but thought better of it. He managed a nod and kept his mouth shut.

"When I hired you, you indicated you had ambitions to progress rapidly on a management track," Carl continued. "To make up for lost time, I believe you said."

"Yes, sir."

"Deviating from company policies is not the behavior of a man who wants to be noticed—and promoted—by those higher up in the company."

"No, sir," Bryan said. He felt like a schoolboy summoned to the principal's office—a feeling he would have thought himself long grown out of by now.

Carl leaned forward and assumed the expression of a concerned father. "I took a risk hiring you, knowing you have a somewhat…unorthodox background. I hope you won't make me disappointed in my decision."

"No, sir." Carl *had* taken a chance hiring him, and Bryan appreciated that. But did that mean he owed the man his soul?

Carl sat back, his expression more congenial. "We all make mistakes, so I'll overlook this transgression. I trust it won't happen again."

"No, sir."

"That's fine. I'm glad we cleared that up." Carl smiled. "Have you reviewed those financial reports I gave you last week?"

"Yes, sir." Determined not to seem like a pouting teenager, Bryan sat up straighter and focused on the reports. "I noticed a few areas where costs seemed to be out of line and I wanted to discuss them with you."

"Excellent. Why don't you write me a report outlining your findings and I'll review it?"

It wasn't the one-on-one discussion he'd hoped for, but Bryan wasn't going to push his luck. He recognized a dismissal when he heard one. "I'll get right on it," he said.

"You do that." Carl nodded, his attention already focused on the computer screen to his right.

Bryan left the office, his expression bland, though inside, he was fuming. This was the part of working for someone else he hated—being called on the carpet and talked to as if he were a stupid child.

He'd meant it when he'd told Carl he wanted to get ahead. The faster he progressed, the more promotions and raises he got, the more he'd learn and save. Every day would bring him closer to opening his own place.

He'd always been stubborn, and now he thought his determination would help him get to where he wanted to be. But if this was the price he had to pay to get what he wanted, it was going to be tougher than he'd imagined.

Chapter Five

When Angela was stressed or upset, she cooked. Big pans of brownies. Pots of soup. Homemade lasagna or meatballs. After she split with Troy she made a complete roast turkey dinner—in the middle of June.

Dancing with Bryan didn't rate a turkey dinner, but homemade meatloaf and mashed potatoes sounded comforting enough to calm her. That wasn't a meal to be eaten alone, however, so she invited Tanya and her daughter for dinner before rehearsal Tuesday evening.

"You said this was just a family supper," Tanya said when Angela led her and Annie into the small front parlor that served as Angela's dining room. "Nothing formal." She stared at the table laid with silver and china. Fresh rolls steamed in a napkin-lined basket, green beans glistening with butter and flecked with chopped almonds waited in a serving bowl beside a second bowl mounded with buttery mashed potatoes. The meatloaf, crisply brown with a cap of red sauce, rested on a platter in the center of the table. "My mother doesn't even get this fancy for Christmas," Tanya said.

"It smells great," Annie said, pulling out a chair on one side of the table.

"Go ahead and have a seat and I'll open the wine," Angela said, taking the bottle Tanya had brought as her contribution to the meal.

"So, what's the occasion?" Tanya asked when Angela returned with the wine and a glass of milk for Annie.

Angela filled their wineglasses, then took her seat at the head of the table. "No special occasion. I just felt like making a nice meal for my favorite director and her daughter."

"Your favorite director appreciates it very much." Tanya took a bite of meatloaf and moaned softly. "This is so good."

"You should open a restaurant," Annie said, happily making patterns in her mashed potatoes with the back of her spoon.

"Crested Butte has enough restaurants. I'll stick to chocolates."

They ate for a while in silence, Annie devouring almost as much as the women. At last Tanya pushed her plate away with a sigh. "I can't remember the last time I ate so well," she said. "Thank you."

"Do we have dessert?" Annie asked.

"There are chocolate cupcakes in the kitchen," Angela said. "Why don't you go help yourself to one and take it in the living room. You can watch TV while your mom and I visit."

"Okay." Annie slipped from her chair and raced to the kitchen.

"She never stops running," Tanya said.

"Maybe she'll be a track star."

"She's already learning to snowboard," Tanya said. "We've been to the slopes a few times and she's pretty good."

"I think you have to learn at that age to be any good."

"Hmm." Tanya sipped her wine. "Speaking of pretty good snowboarders, have you heard from Bryan?"

"No, I haven't heard from him." She would never admit, even to Tanya, how much that bothered her. "Can't I have one dance with a guy without you trying to make something of it?"

"I didn't have to try to make something of it," Tanya said. "It's obvious he's really into you."

"Oh, please!" Angela gulped wine to hide her consternation at this assertion. "Bryan's a nice guy, but he's *not* into me."

"He is."

"You're imagining things. I really don't think I'm his type."

"What type would that be?"

"You know—gorgeous."

"Oh, please! Don't tell me you're one of those women who is all hung up about your looks." Tanya set down her glass with at thump and gave Angela a stern look. "I realize we as women are too often judged by our appearance, but have you checked a mirror lately? You are by no stretch of the imagination ugly. And pretending otherwise is just…well, lame."

"Spoken like a woman who has been gorgeous and slim her whole life."

"So this is a weight thing."

Angela's chair creaked as she shifted position. "What do you mean, a weight thing?"

"You think Bryan—or some other good-looking guy—couldn't appreciate you because you're a little heavier than what society says is the ideal."

"I'm fine with how I look," Angela said. "And I'm sure there are men out there who don't have a problem with a woman having real curves. I'm simply not sure Bryan is one of them."

"Why not?"

"Come on. You've seen the women he dates. Women like Rhiannon—real beauty queens."

Tanya dismissed this idea with a wave of her hand. "Most of them were snowboarders. He was drawing from the women he knew."

"That's even worse. He likes athletic women, and I'm not athletic."

Tanya leaned across the table. "What has gotten into you? You're usually so confident. So comfortable in your own skin. Exactly the kind of woman a lot of guys like."

Angela tried to straighten her shoulders, to hold her head up and regain some of her old poise, but it had deserted her. "I know I'm supposed to be this strong, modern woman, self-confident and sure of my inner beauty, et cetera, et cetera," she said. "But it's not always that easy, you know? Most of the time I can fake it pretty good. Heck, most of the time, I really *do* feel that way. But then something happens—a cute guy like Bryan asks me out— and all the old insecurities and doubts rear up out of their hiding places and reduce me to…to this." She drained her wineglass.

Tanya continued to stare at her. "Bryan asked you out?" she asked after a moment.

Angela nodded.

"You said yes, right?"

"I said no."

"You said no?" Tanya's voice rose.

"I couldn't face the possibility of things not working out between us."

"Are you telling me you're planning the end of the relationship before there's a beginning?"

"I know it *sounds* silly. It *is* silly. But the fear is real, even if the basis for it isn't."

"You *do* like him, don't you?"

"Yes. That's part of the problem. I think it would be really easy for me to fall hard for him." She was halfway there already and they hadn't even dated.

"Would that be so bad?"

"But what happens if he leaves? I don't know if I could go through that again."

Tanya refilled their glasses. "So that's what this is really about—Troy."

"You've been through a big breakup. You know how much it hurts."

Tanya nodded. "I know."

"And it wasn't just that Troy left me, it was the way he did it."

Tanya nodded again. "I know." She sipped her wine and looked thoughtful. "But Bryan isn't Troy."

"He's enough like him that it makes me uneasy. They're both really good looking, used to dating only the best-looking women, always the life of the party. And let's face it—sooner or later someone he knows is going to make some remark like 'what are you doing with *her?*' and he'll start to second guess the attraction. That's what happened with Troy."

"Maybe Bryan is stronger than Troy. Maybe he doesn't care what other people think. Besides, you know they're wrong. You're a gorgeous, sexy woman. Bryan sees that. Who cares about a number on a scale?"

"Some people care. Maybe down inside, Bryan cares."

"That's a big maybe," Tanya said. "I hate to see you lose out on a chance to be happy because of something that may never happen."

Angela nodded. "I want to be strong. To be a risk taker. But I don't know if I can do it."

Tanya looked thoughtful. "What if it were a role onstage?"

"What do you mean?"

"How would you act the part if it were a role onstage?"

"I'd be strong and confident."

"And you'd go out with Bryan."

"Yes. But onstage there wouldn't be any consequences of making the wrong decision. At least, no real ones."

"But in real life you'll have a good time with a great guy. You might even end up living happily ever after."

"That's a big might."

Tanya smiled. "Give it a try. Go after it like a role onstage."

"Sort of fake it till you make it?"

"Right. Pretend you're that strong, confident woman you want to be. Give Bryan a chance to prove what kind of man he really is."

"And if things don't work out?"

"Then come cry on my shoulder and we'll drink some more wine and figure out a new plan." She leaned over and put her hand on Angela's. "I know how tempting it is when you've had a bad experience to draw into yourself and give up on love. But we can't do that. Not unless we want to spend the rest of our lives alone."

"Maybe alone wouldn't be so bad."

"I know you don't mean that."

"You're right. I don't." Angela took a deep breath and imagined herself strong, confident and in charge. "I am woman, hear me roar," she said.

"You don't have to roar," Tanya said. "Just give him an I-want-you smile and the poor man won't know what hit him."

BRYAN SAT AT HIS DESK, staring into space and hoping anyone who passed would think he was contemplating business. In less than two weeks the lifts would shut down for the season and the hotel would lock its doors for a week of deep-cleaning and maintenance. He had a lot to do to get ready for this, but his mind wasn't on work. A spring snow had dumped six inches of fresh powder on the slopes over the weekend. Today the sun was shining and a lot of his friends were out there having a good time while he was stuck behind this desk reviewing occupancy figures and compiling a list of maintenance issues.

Last year at this time, he and Zephyr had spent whole days in the terrain park and on the steeps, reveling in the spring snow and sparse crowds. They'd flirted with pretty girls, planned a trip out of town for April mud season and looked forward to a summer of hiking, biking and having fun. Bryan's job as a night auditor at the hotel hadn't paid much, but it had allowed plenty of free time to do whatever he wanted.

He'd realized taking a full-time job would mean giving all that up, but he hadn't anticipated how hard that would be on days like today.

Rachel leaned into his doorway. "Hey, Bry, I was wondering if we should start cleaning out the lost and found closet?"

"We have a lost and found closet?" He set aside the folder of paperwork and stood, glad to stretch his legs and clear the fog from his brain. "What's in it?"

"Come on and I'll show you." He followed her to the end of the hall, where she opened a door to reveal a space stuffed floor to ceiling with miscellaneous items. "It's all stuff people leave behind in their rooms," Rachel said. She reached in and began pulling out random items. "Pillows, clothes, books. And we have a bunch of hats and gloves and some jackets that get left at the restaurant and bar. We stick everything in the closet in case anyone comes looking for it and we clean it out at the end of the season."

Bryan picked up a pair of fur-lined leather men's gloves. They looked expensive. "What do you do with it all?"

"When this was Club Med, we'd divvy everything up among the staff." She held up a women's sweater and studied it critically. "I got a great leather jacket that way."

"I don't see why we can't do that now." Maybe he'd take these gloves.

"Cool." Rachel draped the sweater over her arm and leaned in to sort through the rest of the contents of the closet. Bryan squeezed in beside her. He was amazed at some of what he found—everything from paperback novels to baby pacifiers. Lots of clothes and toiletries. Several pairs of shoes.

"The housekeeping staff has found sex toys and porn before," Rachel said as she tossed aside an empty canvas duffle bag. "Those go straight into the trash. And anything really valuable like jewelry goes into the safe in the manager's office and he contacts the last occupant of the room about it."

"I can't believe people forget this stuff." He held up a pair of ski goggles. Too small for him.

"Bryan, there you are. I've been looking for you." Bryan and Rachel backed out of the closet and turned to greet Carl. "What are you two doing?" Carl asked.

Scoring booty guests left behind didn't sound like something Carl would appreciate. "We're inventorying the lost and found closet," Bryan said.

Carl glanced into the closet and made a face. "Never mind that. Just box everything up and ship it to the homeless mission in Gunnison."

"Sure thing," Bryan said. "I'll let the staff go through it first and see if there's anything they can use."

"Absolutely not." Carl looked offended by the suggestion.

"Why not? There are some really nice things in here."

"Corporate policy prohibits staff members from retaining any item left behind by guests."

More ridiculously rigid company policy. "That doesn't make any sense," Bryan said. "Why shouldn't the staff get some use out of the items?"

"It makes perfect sense if you think about it," Carl said. "What if you were a guest who misplaced, say, this nice pair of leather gloves." He took the gloves Bryan had been holding. "You don't remember where you left them and you've written them off. Then one day, several months later, you return to the Elevation Hotel, where you enjoyed your last stay, and the bellman is wearing gloves exactly like the pair you lost. You might, not unreasonably, suspect that the gloves had been stolen on your last visit. Even if the guest never said anything to us, it would be unlikely we would have his business again."

"I see what you mean," Bryan admitted. "But how likely is that to happen, really?"

"The possibility is enough to warrant the policy." Carl turned to Rachel. "Box everything up and see that it's delivered to the homeless mission with our compliments."

"Yes, sir."

"Bryan, you come with me."

Reluctantly, Bryan followed his boss to his office. He was beginning to think of the warren of windowless rooms as cells. Though being able to look out at the bright sun on the snow would probably only make him feel worse.

"I understand there's another local festival soon," Phelps said as he settled behind his desk. "Something called Flauschink?"

Bryan sat in a chair across from his boss. "It's a big party to celebrate the closing of the lifts and the flushing out of winter. There's a parade and a costume party. The final weekend here at the resort a lot of people dress in costume, and the king and queen of Flauschink make an appearance at the Ice Bar on Sunday afternoon."

New lines furrowed Carl's brow. "Will it be a rowdy crowd?"

"Not rowdy in a bad way. It used to be a lot wilder, with people skiing naked and stuff like that, but that doesn't really happen anymore."

"Naked skiing? Isn't that terribly cold?"

"Not if you've ingested enough, um, antifreeze." Bryan forced back a grin. He didn't have any *personal* experience, but he knew a few people...

"That sounds like a rowdy crowd to me," Carl said.

"Yeah, but like I said, it doesn't happen anymore. The resort usually has a few cops around to issue tickets to anyone who gets out of hand. Mostly it's about having fun and ending the season in style."

Carl nodded. "You say there's a parade?"

"Yes, down Elk Avenue. Nothing fancy—some floats and people in costume."

"We should have a float. Can you pull something together?"

"Uh, sure." Working on the float sounded better than being stuck in an office. "I've got some friends who can help."

"Do it then. Something to show we're a part of the community. But nothing too outlandish. We want to keep our reputation as a first-class lodging facility."

"Right." He silently vowed that if he ever started referring to the hotel as a lodging facility, he'd ask someone to hit him over the head to knock the pretension right out of him.

Carl nodded in dismissal, and Bryan drifted back to his own desk. Now to come up with a float that fit into

Flauschink's reputation for wackiness without offending Carl's sensibilities. Zephyr and Max would help with construction and logistics, but if Bryan turned those two loose on the design he'd end up with a giant psychedelic toilet or a bunch of clowns wielding plungers—both past entries in Flauschink parades. He needed help from someone with a sense of humor, but also a reputation for class. Someone with a flair for drama and experience putting on a production.

After a moment's thought, he picked up the phone and punched in a number. "Angela, it's Bryan. I know you're busy with the play right now, but I really need your help with a project."

ANGELA AGREED to help Bryan with the float for the Flauschink parade because she was flattered he'd asked her, and because she reasoned it would be a safe way to gradually get used to the possibility of going out with him and becoming something more than friends. They'd be working together, but around other people.

Then she began worrying about the other people. Would Rhiannon be one of those people? Or some other gorgeous young woman who would make Angela look like an Amazon?

Get over it! she scolded herself. Maybe the best thing for her would be for Bryan to see her right alongside the type of women he usually dated. It would either snap him out of whatever fog of attraction he was in, or prove that maybe there was something to the heat they generated whenever they were together.

If nothing else, the float project would add one more thing to her to-do list and keep her too busy to brood over romance. The float group agreed to meet Wednesday, before dress rehearsals for *I Hate Hamlet* on Thursday and the play's opening on Friday. They'd spend several nights the following week putting the float together before the Flauschink parade that Saturday.

Wednesday evening when Angela arrived at the Last Steep, she wasn't surprised to see Zephyr and Max, along with Casey and Trish, seated around a long table with three pizzas and several pitchers of beer in front of them. "You're just in time for chow," Zephyr said, passing her a plate. "Who can come up with good ideas on an empty stomach?"

"Thanks." She took the only empty chair, next to Bryan.

"Is beer okay?" he asked. "I can get you a soda or something."

"Beer is fine." She accepted the glass he poured and tried not to let her eyes linger too long on him. Had it really been more than a week since she'd last seen him? He was dressed casually in jeans and a fleece pullover. If possible, she thought he looked even more handsome than he had in his suit.

"What kind of budget do we have for this float?" Casey asked after they'd all helped themselves to pizza.

"The hotel is paying, but not a lot," Bryan said.

"So, are we talking crepe paper on a pickup truck or ten chorus girls on a flatbed trailer?" Zephyr asked.

"I think we can spring for the trailer," Bryan said. "Minus the chorus girls."

"Too bad," Zephyr said, dodging a blow from Trish.

"I know a guy I can call about a truck and trailer," Max said. "So I can take care of that."

"Did your boss give you any idea what he wants on this float?" Casey asked.

"Nope." Bryan picked a slice of pepperoni off a piece of pizza and popped it in his mouth. "He wants to show the hotel is a part of the community. But we can't get too wild."

"Where's the fun in that?" Zephyr asked.

"Maybe we should start by looking at what other groups are doing with their floats," Trish said. "That might give us some ideas for a theme or something."

"The Chamber is handling all the parade reservations, so I know some of them." Casey wiped her hand on a paper napkin. "There's the usual float with all the former Flauschink kings and queens," she said. "And a convertible with the reigning royalty. There's a float in protest of plans to mine molybdenum on Red Lady."

"I heard about that one," Max said. "They're making a big papier mâché toilet and flushing a mining executive down it."

"No toilets," Trish said. "That's so overdone."

"Flauschink is about *flushing* winter," Zephyr said.

"Do you have any ideas, Angela?" Bryan turned toward her, his knee brushing against her thigh.

She shrugged. "Since it's a commercially sponsored float, why not promote the hotel?"

"That sounds boring," Zephyr said.

"What would we do? Construct a model of the hotel or something?" Casey asked.

"I don't know," Angela said. "What do you think of when you think of the hotel? Or any hotel?"

"Beds," Max said.

"What?" Casey stared at him.

"Beds." Max helped himself to another slice of pizza. "You rent a hotel room for the bed. It's a place to spend the night."

"So we have a float with a bed?" Trish looked doubtful.

"It could work," Angela said. "You could have a couple in old-fashioned night clothes and a big brass bed."

"Ooh, I know!" Casey held up her hand. "We could have

a banner that says *Wake up from your long winter's nap at the Elevation Hotel*."

"And the guy could chase the woman around the bed!" Zephyr said. "I like it."

"I like it, too," Bryan said. "It's funny."

"So, who should we get to dress up in nightclothes and chase each other around the float?" Trish asked. "Bryan, you're the only person here from the hotel. Maybe you should do it."

Bryan shook his head. "No way. Besides, who would I chase?"

"I can think of a few girls who would let you chase them," Zephyr said. "Some of them might even let you catch them. There's Rhiannon and Rachel and— Ouch! Casey, why did you kick me?"

"Why don't we have Casey and Max be the couple?" Angela said, anxious to steer the conversation in a safer direction. Not that she'd be caught dead in a voluminous nightgown and frilly cap on a float in broad daylight, but she had no intention of watching Bryan chase anyone else around in her place.

"Yeah, I guess so," Zephyr said. "They're married and all, so nobody can complain we're being immoral."

"We don't plan on doing anything immoral," Casey protested.

"At least not when anyone's around to see," Max added.

"The prop department at the theater might have a bed we can use," Angela said.

"I'll ask around about costumes," Casey said.

"I'm not wearing a nightshirt," Max said. "I'd look ridiculous."

"What are you going to wear?" Bryan asked.

"I've got a pair of old-fashioned, long-handle underwear,"

he said. "I'll wear those and some wild socks and maybe a stocking cap."

"Be still my heart," Casey said.

"Ah, you know you'll love it."

"Only because I love you."

"Now that we've got that out of the way—" Zephyr rubbed his hands together "—what's everybody doing for mud season?"

After the lifts closed, the piles of snow around town began to melt, turning the streets into muddy quagmires. The winter tourists departed and the summer tourists hadn't yet arrived, so business was slow. Those who could afford to do so left town for warmer, drier climes.

"Casey and I are headed back east to visit my folks," Max said.

"I'm going to Broomfield to see my mom for a week," Angela said. She would have preferred a week in Hawaii, but her budget and family duty dictated a week in the Denver suburb instead.

"You people are so boring," Zephyr said. "Trish and I are going to Moab for a week of biking, hiking and soaking up the sun."

Angela turned to Bryan. "What are you doing for mud season?" she asked.

"Working," he said. "Carl's going to a conference in St. Louis, so I'm in charge while he's away."

"Watch out, it's the boss!" Zephyr put up his hands in mock fear. "I'll be thinking of you, stuck in the five-day-a-week grind while I'm barreling over those red rock single-tracks, bro."

"You do that," Bryan said drily.

"I have to go now," Zephyr said, standing. "Moose Juice is rehearsing tonight. We're playing at LoBar Saturday night."

"If you don't need us for anything else, we'll be going, too," Max said, helping Casey with her coat.

"No, we're good." Bryan stood. "Let's meet back here next Wednesday and coordinate everything for Saturday."

Goodbyes were exchanged and within minutes Angela and Bryan were alone at the table with a stack of plates and empty pizza boxes. "Thanks for coming out to help us," he said. "I knew you'd have good ideas."

"Thanks for inviting me. I've been saying I should get out more with non-theater people. Expand my social circle."

He shifted in his chair. "What Zephyr was saying, about those women wanting me to chase them. Don't pay any attention to that. He's full of it."

"I don't think he's so far wrong, really," she said. "You have a reputation as a popular guy."

He flushed to the tips of his ears, a reaction that only endeared him to her more. It would be so much easier to resist him if he were vain or more of a braggart. Then again, she probably wouldn't have ever been attracted to a man like that.

"I guess I have dated a lot of women, but I was never serious about any of them," he said.

"You don't have to justify yourself to me," she said. "Honestly."

She started to move away from the table, but he blocked her path. "But I feel I do," he said. "I don't want you thinking I'm some slacker playboy. Yeah, I used to live that life, but I'm headed in a different direction now. Working at the Elevation is only the beginning. I have plans. I'm not a slacker, and I'm not a corporate drone who plans to sit behind a desk the rest of my life."

"I don't think that about you."

"Then what *do* you think?"

She felt flustered, put on the spot. How honest could she afford to be? "I think you're a smart, hard-working, ambitious guy. You're good-looking, but you're not vain about it. You're loyal to your friends. You have a good sense of humor. You're really nice."

"Nice." He spoke the word as if it was a curse.

"Niceness is underrated," she said. "There's too much meanness in the world, so when I say nice, I mean it as a real compliment. Now, I really do have to go."

She moved past him. This time he didn't try to stop her, though she could feel his gaze on her as she hurried across the room and out the door.

Coward, she scolded herself as she jammed her keys in the ignition of her car. *Why didn't you stick around and ask him what he thought of you?*

Because as much as she could be brave in the make-believe world onstage, reality often left her shaking in her shoes.

She didn't know which would be more terrifying—hearing that Bryan thought of her as just a girl he could have a few laughs with…or that he wanted much more.

Chapter Six

Friday afternoon found Bryan checking the time every ten minutes, anxious to be out of the office for the weekend. The toughest thing wasn't dealing with hotel guests, navigating office politics or even pretending to laugh at Carl's jokes; it was having to show up every day, all day, subject to the company's schedule. Years of freedom on the slopes hadn't prepared him for such restraints. As five o'clock slowly ticked closer he began gathering his belongings, ready to make a quick escape.

At ten minutes to five, Rachel strolled into the office. "Some friends and I are going into Gunni tonight to party," she said, leaning one hip against his desk and fixing him with a provocative smile. "Want to come along?"

"Thanks, but I've got other plans." He pretended to focus on the spreadsheet on the computer screen in front of him, hoping she'd take the hint.

"Do you have a hot date? Someone new I don't know about?"

"No, I don't have a date."

"I'm sure we could fix that." She leaned over and peered at the computer screen.

"I'm not interested." He kept his eyes focused on the spreadsheet, though he could have been looking at Sanskrit for all he really saw of what was there.

"Hmmph." She straightened. "This job sure has changed you."

The words stung. "What do you mean?"

"You used to never pass up a chance to party. You were so much fun. Now you never want to do anything. You're boring."

First nice, now boring. At this rate, no one would believe he'd ever been a chick magnet. "Sorry to disappoint you," he said drily, and began shutting down the computer. He glanced at the clock. Two minutes to five. "I really have to go now."

On her way out of the office, Rachel almost collided with Carl. "Bryan, I'm glad I caught you before you left," the manager said. "I need you to stay late."

Bryan stifled a groan. "What's wrong?" he asked.

"We have a tour group from Japan coming in this afternoon. They were supposed to be here by four, but their plane has been delayed and now they won't be here until six. I need you to stay to greet them and make sure they have everything they need."

Bryan's stomach churned. "Can't the front desk handle that?"

Carl shook his head. "These are executives with a resort development firm from Hokkaido. We want to treat them like VIPs and that means personal service from a manager." He checked his watch. "I'd stay, but my wife's parents are coming in from Detroit and I have to be at the Gunnison airport in less than an hour to pick them up."

"Of course I'll stay," Bryan said, swallowing his disappointment. "I'll make sure to roll out the red carpet."

"Great." Carl clapped him on the shoulder. "I'll check on them tomorrow. My in-laws want to get in some skiing while they're here. You have a good weekend."

"You, too," Bryan said. Though this wasn't the start he'd pictured.

The Japanese VIPs arrived at six-fifteen. By the time Bryan had bowed and shaken hands and escorted them personally to their block of rooms overlooking the slopes, it was almost seven. He practically ran from the hotel and drove as fast as he dared down the mountain toward Crested Butte.

Parking on Elk Avenue was nonexistent; he had to park several blocks away and walk back to the Mallardi Cabaret. He hurried to the lobby and handed over his ticket, then slipped into the theater. The first act of *I Hate Hamlet* was already underway, and he found a seat near the back.

Angela was onstage, almost unrecognizable in her character of a matronly real estate agent. She had the audience's full attention and delivered her comic lines with perfect timing. Bryan watched her, riveted. The woman onstage—a plump, somewhat dowdy older woman full of cynicism and wisecracks—was nothing like the attractive, fashionable, warm and sensual woman he knew. This ability to transform herself intrigued him.

At intermission, he joined the throng of people in the lobby. He was sipping a cup of lukewarm punch when someone jostled his elbow. "Bryan, my man!" Zephyr clapped his hand on Bryan's shoulder. "I didn't know you'd be here."

Dressed in faded maroon cords, a well-worn, brown leather bomber jacket and a black T-shirt advertising his band, Moose Juice—illustrated with a large, drooling moose—Zephyr definitely stood out in the sweaters-and-jeans crowd. For that matter, Bryan's suit was a little out of place, though he saw a few men in sports coats, and several women in nice dresses.

"What are you doing here?" Bryan asked. He'd never pictured Zephyr as a fan of live theater.

"Trish is trying to teach me culture," he said.

The woman in question approached and handed Zephyr a cup of punch. "Plus, we got free tickets," she said. "What are *you* doing here?"

"After working with the theater people on the fund-raiser, I wanted to see what all the fuss was about," he said.

Trish's gaze remained fixed on him with all the intensity of a missile-guiding laser. "Uh-huh. And are you enjoying the play?"

"Yeah, I am. It's funny and the actors do a good job."

"Angela and Tanya in particular," Trish said. "They're very talented."

"Yeah, and Tanya is hot," Zephyr said.

Trish glared at him and his grin faded. "Not as hot as you, babe," he said, and put his arm around her.

Mollified, Trish turned to Bryan again. "There's a little party after the show. The actors and their friends. You should stop by."

"Maybe I will," he said.

"Yeah," Zephyr said. "You can get to know Tanya better. Maybe ask her out— Hey!" He dodged a sharp poke from Trish's elbow. "I'm just trying to help out a friend," he protested. "He said he wanted to find someone to settle down with. Tanya's got a kid. That sounds pretty settled to me." He winked at Bryan. "And I think she's your type."

"What, exactly, is my type?" Bryan asked.

"Dude, you don't know?"

"I want to know what *you* think is my type."

"Easy." Zephyr held up one hand and began counting off on his fingers. "She has to be smart. You never went for dumb blondes. She has to have a sense of humor, 'cause you're a fun guy. She has to have her own money. Not as important now that you're so gainfully employed, but always a plus. And she has to be a looker, natch."

"Of course." Trish rolled her eyes. "You men!"

"What?" Zephyr gave her a hurt look. "Don't tell me you weren't attracted to me because of my looks."

"Guess again, hotshot." She looked at Bryan thoughtfully. "Actually, I think when Bryan falls in love, it will be with someone he never expected to be attracted to," she said. "Someone he never thought of as his type at all."

"Nah!" Zephyr protested. "Why do you think that?"

She smiled at him. "What do you think happened with me?" She tugged at his arm. "Come on, it's time to get back to our seats. See you later, Bryan."

"Yeah. See ya." Bryan tossed his cup in the trash and returned to his seat, pondering Zephyr's list of requirements for Bryan's right woman. Angela was smart, funny, and she had her own successful business. That left *a looker*. According to Zephyr—and if Bryan was honest, himself before he met her—Angela didn't qualify under the standard definition. Lookers were fashion models, cheerleaders or women who could be. The kind of women Bryan had always dated before.

And yet, Angela was beautiful. She had real curves and an earthy sensuality that left him a little breathless whenever he was near her. So—smart, funny, successful and beautiful. The perfect woman for him. The idea made him a little light-headed. Angela wouldn't even go out with him. He obviously wasn't *her* ideal.

The play resumed and once more Bryan was caught up in

the performance. When it ended, he stood with the rest of the audience to applaud while the actors took their bows. When Angela stepped forward, he let out an enthusiastic whistle, causing heads around him to turn. Let them wonder.

While the crowd surged toward the exit doors, he fought his way upstream toward backstage. He found Angela there with a group of women. "Angela, that was great," he said when he'd made his way to her side.

She turned to him, eyes glowing. "Bryan! I didn't know you were here."

"I wouldn't have missed it," he said. "You get my vote for best actress."

She laughed. "I'll tell the Academy to give you a call."

"We'll see you at the party, Angela," one of the women said, and the others agreed, then wandered off, leaving Bryan and Angela alone as the area emptied.

"I'm glad you came to the show," she said.

"I almost didn't make it. I had to work late and missed a few minutes of the first act."

"Is this the first time you've been to the Cabaret?" she asked.

"Yes. Shame on me, I guess. I never thought about it much until I met you."

"I have to get out of this makeup, but a bunch of us are having a little get-together at Austin Davies's house in C.B. South," she said. "Would you like to come?"

He told himself she was inviting him solely as a friend— the way she would have invited anyone she knew who stopped backstage after the show. But he wasn't going to pass up the opportunity to spend more time with her. "I would," he said.

"Good. I'll meet you in the parking lot in about twenty

minutes. We can take my car—there isn't a lot of parking and he's asking people to share rides."

"I'll be waiting for you." He couldn't remember when he'd so looked forward to spending time with a woman. Maybe it was because he sensed Angela holding herself back from him that made him so interested in pursuing her. Was it only a case of wanting what he couldn't have?

Or did something more lie at the heart of his attraction to the woman who was as sweet and complex as any of her decadent chocolate creations?

AUSTIN DAVIES LIVED in a two-story, modern, cedar and glass chalet in Crested Butte South. By the time Angela and Bryan arrived, the house was already crowded with people. As they squeezed past clusters of partygoers, working their way farther inside, Angela was acutely aware of the man at her side. Opening nights always had a heady effect on her. The audience's response to her performance had left her unable to stop smiling, feeling almost as if she were floating on their accolades. But when Bryan had come backstage to greet her, to tell her how wonderful *he* thought she'd been, she'd felt as elated as if she'd been awarded a Tony or an Emmy.

She blamed this giddiness for her impulsive invitation to him to join her. The crowd at the party would allow her to enjoy the pleasure of being around him without the danger that she'd say or do something to reveal the intensity of her attraction to him. The truth was she'd scarcely stopped thinking about the man since the first day he called her on the phone. She'd managed to combine the fixation of a schoolgirl crush with a mature woman's out-and-out lust. This dangerous combination meant dating the man was out of the question. If the two of them spent any significant time alone, she might very well self-combust, and the possibility that he might reject her advances was too painful to risk.

"Should we get something to eat?" Bryan asked. "I didn't have a chance to grab dinner before the show."

"I never eat before a performance," she said. "Now I'm starved."

One good thing about having a leading man with money: you could count on a good spread at the after-party. Austin had hired a caterer, who had laid out a gourmet feast. Angela and Bryan filled their plates with hot artichoke dip, bacon-wrapped shrimp, skewered chicken, meatballs and mini quiches. Suddenly, Angela was ravenous. She had an entire mini quiche in her mouth when she realized Bryan was watching her.

So much for any illusions he might have had that she was anything close to dainty. The women he dated probably nibbled around the edges of finger sandwiches and sipped white wine spritzers instead of inhaling plates of food like a hog at the trough. She managed to swallow the quiche and wiped her fingers on a napkin. "I didn't realize how hungry I was until I saw the food," she mumbled.

"It's good, isn't it?" He shoved a whole quiche into his mouth and nodded enthusiastically as he chewed.

Was he making fun of her? She searched his eyes, but saw no hint of mockery.

They moved away from the table and almost collided with Tanya. She'd exchanged the red sequined cocktail dress she wore in her role as Felicia for a black cowl-necked sweater and black jeans and boots. Angela eyed the attractive man trailing her friend. He looked familiar, but she couldn't quite place him.

"This is my brother, Ian," Tanya said, solving the mystery.

"It's nice to meet you, Ian," Angela said, shaking his hand.

"Mom and Dad are around here somewhere," Tanya said, searching the crowd.

"I'll go look for them," Ian said. He nodded to Angela and Bryan, then moved away, and was swallowed by the crowd.

"Did you really bring your brother as your date to this party?" Angela asked, giving Tanya a stern look.

"Our whole family came together," Tanya said. "Except Annie. She's with a sitter." She turned to Bryan. "It's good to see you again," she said.

"The play was terrific," Bryan said. "You did a great job."

"Angela's the real star." Tanya squeezed Angela's arm. "My role is easy compared to hers."

"She is terrific, isn't she?" Bryan's smile was as bright as any spotlight and made Angela feel just as warm.

"Thank you," she murmured.

"It was good to see you." Tanya squeezed her arm again. "I have to go rescue Mom and Dad from one of Austin's monologues."

"Tanya seems really nice," Bryan said when she had moved out of earshot.

"She is," Angela agreed. "She's also gorgeous and talented and really smart. I can't understand why she's still single."

"Maybe she likes it that way," Bryan said. "Not everyone wants to pair up, you know."

"I don't think Tanya is alone because she prefers that," Angela said. "And I know guys ask her out all the time, but for some reason, she's never hit it off with anyone."

"Maybe she's waiting for the one right person," he said. He took her elbow and began steering her through the crowd once more.

"Where are we going?" she asked.

"Somewhere we can sit and talk. It's really crowded in here."

"Come on." She pulled him toward an archway. "I think there's a library or den through here." She tried to recall the layout of the house from previous theater parties. They passed groups of familiar faces and exchanged hellos, but didn't stop. Finally, they came to another archway, one that led to a room filled with bookcases and comfortable furniture. One end was dominated by a large, flat-panel television, which at the moment was switched off.

"We can sit here," Angela said. She set her half-full plate of food on the coffee table and settled onto a chintz-covered loveseat.

Bryan sat beside her. "I never realized before how many people were associated with the theater," he said.

"Oh, everyone here isn't part of the group," she said. "A lot of them are friends or family, or simply people who enjoy a good party."

He smiled. "Like me."

While he finished off the food on his plate and looked around the room, Angela studied him out of the corner of her eye. On closer inspection, he wasn't movie star handsome. His eyebrows were a little too thick, and his nose a bit too narrow. But there was an arresting quality to his face, a liveliness in his eyes and warmth in his smile that drew people to him. Especially women. "Do women hit on you a lot?" she asked.

He coughed, choking on a cracker, then hastily took a drink.

"What kind of a question is that?" he asked.

"I was just wondering if that kind of thing is the same for

men and women. Not that I've had experience," she hastened to add, "but I know guys hit on Tanya all the time."

"Um, I guess I never thought about it much," he said, looking sheepish.

She laughed. "They probably do, but what guy is going to complain? Am I right?"

He shook his head. "Maybe you could say I'm getting more particular as I get older."

"Particular?"

"I guess that's what you'd call it. There are types of women I used to go for who don't interest me so much anymore." His eyes met hers and she felt a jolt of renewed heat. The message he was sending was clear enough—that he could go for her. She just didn't understand why a guy like him was looking at *her* that way.

He was the first to look away and she let out the breath she hadn't even realized she'd been holding. She liked that she'd unsettled him a little, thrown him off balance. It made her feel more in control of her own feelings. "You said maybe Tanya is waiting for the one right person," she said. "Do you really believe there's only one right person for each of us?"

"Maybe not for everybody, but for some people, yeah." His gaze met hers, serious and intense. "Is it so crazy to think that some people are drawn to each other because they're meant to be together?"

So much for being in control of her feelings. Right now, her heart was racing so hard she fully expected that if she looked down she'd see the ruffles at the neck of her blouse fluttering from the vibrations. Was Bryan trying to tell her something, or was she reading more than she should into his look? "It's a nice idea, isn't it?" she said, keeping her voice light. "Tell me more about this idea of there being types of women. What types of women do you categorize?"

"I can't give away all my secrets," he said. "It would go against the code."

"The code?"

"The man code. All the things we're sworn not to reveal to the opposite sex."

"When do you swear this? Is there some ceremony I don't know about?"

He looked very serious. "Women aren't supposed to know about it. It involves guy stuff—beer and dirt and blood and stuff."

"I'll bet there's a clubhouse and a no girls allowed sign, too."

"You've obviously been spying."

She laughed and without thought, put a hand on his arm. His muscles tensed beneath her fingers, and he turned toward her and covered her hand with his own. "I love to hear you laugh," he said.

The sound caught in her throat. She froze, mesmerized by the intensity of his gaze. She wanted to tell him how easy it was to laugh when she was with him. How tempting it was to let down her guard with him in spite of all her insecurities.

"There's something I've really been wanting to do," he said.

"What's that?"

He took her drink from her hand and set it on the coffee table. "This." He leaned closer and his lips touched hers, warm and firm.

Chapter Seven

Angela gave a small cry of surprise, but made no move to pull away. In fact, she leaned toward Bryan and put one hand on his shoulder, as if to steady herself—or to keep him from leaving her.

He deepened the kiss, and with a second sigh she relaxed into his caress, eyes closed, every sense focused on the feel of his mouth against hers. He kissed with the intensity of a man determined to savor every sensation, his mouth moving gently against hers. His tongue touched her lips and she opened to him, inviting him in. She tasted the sweet malt of beer and felt his heat flowing into her, warming her. She kneaded the hard muscle of his shoulder, as if clinging to him allowed her to hold on to some semblance of control. But she'd been in control—and alone—for so many years now. The idea of abandoning herself to this heady mixture of lust and longing tempted her mightily.

Then he lifted his head and drew back. She opened her eyes and found him watching her, like a man who was trying to decide if he'd made a mistake or not. "What?" she asked. "Why are you looking at me that way?"

"I'm waiting to see if you're going to slap me."

His answer was so unexpected, she choked back a laugh. "If you thought I'd slap you, why did you kiss me?"

"Some things are worth taking a chance on."

"So you think that kiss was worth the risk."

"Yes. Don't you?"

She wet her lips, which still felt hot and sensitive. "Yes. Yes, I do. And I won't slap you."

"Then maybe we should try again." He leaned toward her once more, but loud voices in the hallway made them freeze, then draw apart.

"What are you two doing hiding in here?" Zephyr entered the room, followed by Trish. Face flushed, dreadlocks sticking out at wild angles, Zephyr looked like a man who'd been enjoying himself quite a bit. He sank into a chair opposite the loveseat and grinned at them. "What are you two up to?"

Bryan and Angela exchanged glances. *What were they up to, indeed,* she wondered. Had they just exchanged a harmless, enjoyable kiss, or did Bryan mean for this to be the beginning of something more?

And how much more? On the relationship scale, a kiss could mean everything from friends with benefits to the beginning of true love. In her experience, it wasn't always easy to determine where the man intended for things to end up. Another one of those secrets of the man code that weren't revealed to women.

Mistaking physical attraction for true love had gotten her into trouble before, but she didn't want to make the mistake of not taking Bryan seriously if he was. Aargh. It was enough to make a woman want to tear her hair out—or the man's.

She watched as he laughed and joked with Zephyr, and she fixed a pleasant smile on her own face as Trish addressed her. And here she thought her greatest roles had all been on the stage. Pretending indifference while her heart was racing so wildly from the aftereffects of Bryan's kiss was a true test of her acting abilities.

WHILE BRYAN CHATTED with Zephyr and Trish, he was acutely aware of the woman beside him. Every time he turned toward her, the faint aroma of her perfume tickled his senses. Had the others noted her flushed cheeks and slightly swollen lips? And what must his own face look like, though he struggled not to betray his emotions.

The kiss affected him more than he'd expected. He'd intended the moment to be playful, an overture to a renewed effort to convince her to go out with him. Instead, as soon as their lips touched he'd felt her tremble. Such vulnerability in a woman who seemed so strong surprised and touched him. He'd started to pull away, and then she'd leaned into him. Her lips had parted, inviting him in, and he'd felt her yearning, and answered it with a desire of his own.

The heat of that moment burned through him still. Zephyr was his best friend, but his interruption couldn't have been more ill timed. All Bryan wanted was to be alone with Angela, to explore the feelings between them further.

He told himself he'd have plenty of time. They'd ridden to the party together and would eventually leave together. Then, before she left him at his car, he'd convince her that they owed it to themselves to explore their feelings.

"Have you seen the outfit Max came up with for the Flauschink parade float?" Zephyr asked.

Bryan shook his head. "He said something about a pair of long johns."

"Not just any long johns," Trish said. "These are bright red, with a flap in the back."

"Casey knitted him this long, red-and-white striped nightcap," Zephyr said. "It rules! He says he's going to wear it to the polka party the night before."

Polka was only one of the wacky traditions associated with Flauschink. The ball was the first public appearance of the Flauschink king and queen, who ruled over the festivities with their toilet plunger scepters. Their loyal subjects attended the ball in costume. "What are you going as?" Bryan asked.

"Trish and I wanted to come up with coordinating costumes," Zephyr said.

"I suggested we go as a horse," Trish said. "He could be the back half."

Zephyr ignored this dig. "We decided to go as Mr. and Mrs. Yeti," he said.

"Mrs. Yeti looks just like Mr. Yeti, except she has false eyelashes and a wreath of flowers on her head," Trish said. "Although I have to admit, the costumes I found look more like shaggy polar bears."

"That sounds hilarious," Angela said, laughing. She turned to Bryan. "What's your costume going to be?"

He'd been too busy to even think about the ball. "You first," he said. "Or are you going as your character in *I Hate Hamlet?*"

"I can't go to the ball," she said. "I promised Tanya I'd babysit."

"Too bad," Zephyr said. "It's always a great party. So 'fess up, Bry. What's your costume this year?" Not waiting for an answer, he turned to Angela. "He always comes up with the craziest costumes. One year, he and I came as Cheech and Chong—you know, the pot-smoking hippie dudes that were popular back in my mom and dad's day. Another year, Bryan wore a lampshade on his head. He carried this huge martini glass, taped confetti all over his body, and wore a sign that said 'The Life of the Party.' It was so perfect."

Angela studied him, a faint smile on her face. "I'd like to have seen that."

"I'm sure somebody has pictures somewhere," Zephyr said. "I could ask around."

"Don't bother," Bryan said.

"You still haven't told us what your costume's gonna be this year," Zephyr said.

"I might stay home this year," Bryan said. If Angela wasn't going to be there, why bother?

"That's certainly not like you," Trish said.

"Yeah, you never miss a party, dude."

When would people stop seeing him as a slacker who was only out for a good time? "There's more to life than parties," he said.

"You're working too hard," Zephyr said. "Phelps is a slave driver."

"No, he's not. It takes a lot to keep a big hotel going. I'm learning how much."

"You're not having fun doing it," Zephyr said.

"Life's not just about having fun," Bryan snapped. He was tired of Zephyr giving him a hard time about his decision to change his life. Why couldn't his friend accept him without judging him?

"Hey, chill," Zephyr said. "What's gotten into you?"

Bryan rubbed his head, where the beginning of a headache pounded. "Nothing." He stood. "Maybe I just need some air."

He gave a half-hearted wave goodbye, then left the room.

Angela came after him. "Are you okay?" she asked, touching his shoulder.

"I'm sorry I snapped at Zephyr," he said. "I didn't mean to put a damper on the evening."

"It's okay," she said. "I'm tired, too. Maybe we should go."

"If you're sure you don't mind."

She nodded. "I'm ready to leave. Really."

They said their goodbyes, collected their coats and left. In Angela's car, darkness and silence surrounded them. The lights of distant houses glowed like fireflies among the dark pines up against the shadowed slopes of the mountains. Only a handful of stars showed in the sky, glittering like shards of broken glass.

Bryan stared at these pinpricks of light and tried to think of some way to bring up the kiss he and Angela had shared. Maybe it hadn't affected her the way it had him. Maybe the attraction was all one-sided.

But no, he couldn't be wrong about that. She'd melted in his arms, soft and pliant and tempting as the rich fudge that drew people to her store.

She cleared her throat. "About that kiss—"

"It was an amazing kiss," he said, turning toward her.

She gripped the steering wheel more firmly and kept her eyes focused straight ahead. "Yes. Yes, it was."

"Then you agree there's something between us. Something special."

She hesitated, as if debating her answer. "I know I'm very attracted to you," she said finally.

"I've been attracted to you since the first day I saw you."

"You have?" She glanced at him. "Why? I mean, I'm not saying I don't have my charms, but I'm not the type to turn most men's heads."

Was she being overly modest, or did she really think that? "You turned my head. I can't explain it. I just... Maybe some things are beyond explaining. I wasn't looking for anyone and then…there you were."

She smiled, some of the tension draining from her face. "I never realized you were such a romantic."

"I'm not. Not really." He ran his hand through his hair, struggling to get the right words out. "I guess lately I'm finding out all kinds of new things about myself."

"What kind of things?" she asked.

"How I like my job, for one. Even the boring parts. I like it because it's getting me closer to my dream. For the first time in a long time, instead of just letting life happen to me, I'm making things happen."

She pulled to the curb behind his parked car. When she'd shut off the engine, she turned to him. "What is your dream?" she asked.

"I want to own a boutique inn," he said without hesitation. "An exclusive place that would specialize in luxury accommodations, gourmet food and personal service. More than a bed-and-breakfast but much smaller than the Elevation. Maybe twenty or thirty rooms with a restaurant and bar and some meeting rooms for conferences or weddings and other events."

"You've really thought this out, haven't you?"

"I've been thinking about it for years. I've spent hours online, researching similar places in the U.S. and Europe. I've thought about how to market it, where to get the money to start. But I knew I needed more experience in the business side of things. And I needed to earn the cash to put into property. This job at the Elevation is giving me that."

"It sounds wonderful. I know you'll do a great job."

"You have your own business. You know what it's like to take an idea and make it a reality."

She nodded. "It can be pretty scary sometimes. But rewarding, too."

"You understand. That's another thing I like about you."

She smiled, though she still looked shaky. "When you say things like that, I really do think you're perfect."

The words sent a nervous shudder through him. "I don't know about perfect," he said. "But I think we ought to take these feelings and see where they lead."

Her smile vanished once more. "I don't know if I'm ready for that."

"Why not? Are you hung up on all the talk about my partying past?" He scowled. "I'm not like that anymore."

"No, it's not that!" The idea clearly shocked her. "I don't see you that way at all."

"Then what's the problem?"

"It's just—" She rubbed her palms up and down the steering wheel. "You could have any woman in town you want. I've seen the way they act around you. You're good-looking and charming and—"

"But I don't want any of those women. I want you."

She dropped her hands to her lap. "I guess I'm having a hard time believing that."

"Then let me prove it." He unsnapped his seat belt and moved over to her. Gently, he turned her head toward his and kissed her again.

At the touch of her lips, he felt her surrender, the stiffness going out of her shoulders. She slid her arms around him and pulled him close, her breasts soft against his chest. He ran one hand down her side, tracing the curve of her hip, then braced his hand against the driver's side door to lean even closer.

The steering wheel jabbed him in the back, and one hand

got tangled in her seat belt. It was a ridiculous position to be in, and yet he didn't care. Making out in the front seat of her car, the windows fogging around him, felt dangerous and exciting in spite of the physical awkwardness.

They finally broke the kiss, breathing hard. "Maybe we'd better stop now," she said.

"Yeah." He disentangled himself and sat back, a little disoriented by the direction the evening had taken. "Can I see you again soon?"

"You'll see me when we work on the float, and again at the Flauschink parade."

Her deliberate avoidance of the real question annoyed him. "You know that's not what I mean."

"I know." She touched the back of his hand. "I shouldn't play games. I want to be honest with you."

"Good. We should be honest with each other."

"Then give me a little more time." She squeezed his hand. "I need to get used to the idea of us as a couple—and to other people seeing us that way."

Bryan knew what it was like to be judged on appearances or first impressions. Too many people still saw him as a ski bum. Now that he was trying to take his life in a new direction, he was finding out how hard it was to change others' expectations. In his case, their judgment made him want to try harder to prove the skeptics wrong; maybe Angela needed more time to get to that place.

"All right." He leaned over to kiss her forehead, then backed away, out of the car. Any more time in her arms and he wouldn't leave at all.

FROM SUNDAY THROUGH Wednesday, Angela alternately congratulated herself for not rushing into anything and berated herself for being a coward. This inability to fix her feelings in one direction infuriated her. She was *not* an indecisive person. At her business and at the theater, she never had trouble choosing a course of action and following it. She was a strong, mature, sensible woman.

Then Bryan walked into her life and every insecurity and weakness she thought she'd long since outgrown came welling up again, like instant adolescence. She wouldn't have been surprised if she woke up some morning soon with a bad case of acne and a burning desire to hang a poster of a young movie star on her wall.

What had she been thinking, telling Bryan she needed more time? More time for what? To convince herself that the feelings she had for him were real and would last? To persuade him that the two of them together would be a mistake?

But how could that kiss be a mistake?

He'd caught her by surprise at the party. When his lips first touched hers, she'd thought maybe she was hallucinating. Something in the wine had induced this too-vivid fantasy and in a moment she'd come to her senses and realize Bryan hadn't kissed her, he'd merely leaned over to pick a stray bit of artichoke dip off her blouse.

But no, he really was kissing her—a hot, luxurious kiss that touched every part of her. Even the memory of it could have thawed ice. This wasn't an ordinary first kiss, tentative or clumsy or casual. It was a heat-seeking missile of a kiss, and it had definitely found its target with her. This was a kiss that said *I'm really into you* in bold, capital letters.

But hadn't she thought the same about Troy? That he was really into her? That he meant it when he said he loved her?

She'd been so sure of her feelings for Troy—sure enough

to accept his proposal of marriage, willing to change her whole life because he'd said he loved her. And in the end she'd been so wrong.

Bryan said he believed in finding the one right person. The concept of soul mates was alluringly romantic. All a woman had to do was find the right person as a partner and all her problems would be solved. Some mystical element—fate or destiny or whatever it was called—would keep her and her lover together without any real work on their part.

Right. That had to be a bigger fairy tale than the one about geese who laid golden eggs or dwarves who did all the housework.

Every relationship took work to get to the happily ever after. The secret was finding a partner to work with you, not against you. Was Bryan that kind of partner, or just another handsome face who would leave her when the sizzle wore off their attraction? People were fond of assuring others that when true love came their way, they'd *know*. As if love could be measured like the soft-boil temperature of candy or the doneness of cake. But how much could you know? How sure could you be? Really.

Right now all Angela knew was that Bryan made her feel giddy and vulnerable and not at all like herself. She knew she wanted him, but she also knew she didn't want to be hurt by him.

WEDNESDAY, ANGELA JOINED Max, Casey, Trish, Zephyr and Bryan in the alley behind Max's snowboard shop to work on their Flauschink float. Bryan's boss from the hotel stopped by briefly. He studied the twin-size brass bed they'd borrowed from the prop department at the theater. "We don't have brass beds at the Elevation Hotel," Carl said.

"It's not meant to be an actual bed from the hotel," Bryan said. "It represents the *idea* of coming to the hotel to spend a night."

Mr. Phelps's frown didn't relax. "And you say you're going to have a young man and woman in their nightclothes, chasing each other around the bed? Isn't that a bit risqué?"

"Old-fashioned nightclothes," Bryan said. "It'll be funny, not off-color. You'll see."

"Perhaps we should use an actual bed from the hotel, with no people," Carl said. "I suppose the banner's okay." He looked to the banner Zephyr and Max had painted: Wake Up From Your Long Winter's Nap at the Elevation Hotel.

"Carl! Dude!" Zephyr put his arm around the hotel manager's shoulder. "What you're suggesting is great, but it's too subtle and sophisticated for this audience. You're aiming for the Bergman film festival crowd. Flauschink is more Three Stooges retrospective. Humor is the way to go here."

Phelps looked stunned, but whether by Zephyr's sudden chumminess or his breath, Angela couldn't be sure. "So you don't think people will get the wrong idea if we have the man chasing the woman around the bed?" he asked.

"Sometimes I'll chase Max instead," Casey spoke up. "It'll be an equal opportunity float."

"People will love it," Bryan said. "They'll remember it. And that's what we want, right? For them to remember the Elevation Hotel next time they need a place to stay, for themselves or for friends or relatives."

Carl's expression relaxed. "All right. I suppose it will be okay. But keep it tasteful."

"We will," Bryan said. Everyone nodded solemnly, though Angela wondered if *tasteful* was quite the way to describe Max's long underwear with the flap in the back.

While Bryan was busy saying goodbye to his boss, and Zephyr and Max covered the base of the trailer with a paper skirt, Angela stuck close to Trish and Casey, making up the bed and decorating it with crepe paper streamers and flowers. Casey had borrowed a bearskin rug from the Chamber of Commerce offices and they spread this alongside the bed, tacking it down with carpet tape to keep it from blowing away.

When they were done, Casey plopped onto the bed. "This is pretty comfy," she said, lying back.

"Oh, yeah." Max stretched out beside her, then rolled toward her. "Maybe Phelps is right. Maybe this is a little risqué." He started nuzzling her neck. She squealed and pushed him away.

"None of that, kids." Zephyr hopped up onto the trailer and shook his finger at them. "Save it for after the parade's over."

"What are you going to wear as your costume?" Trish asked Casey. "Do you have long johns to match Max's?"

Casey grinned. "My costume's a surprise."

"I hope it's risqué," Zephyr said. "Something to make Phelps's eyes pop."

"That would be funny," Bryan said, joining them. "I'd be laughing right up until he fired me."

"If he's that much of a stick-in-the-mud, why would you want to work for him anyway?" Zephyr said.

Bryan frowned at his friend, but said nothing. Angela wondered if Bryan's sudden urge for respectability had caused tension between the two pals.

"Help me tack this banner in place, Bry," Trish said, breaking the staring contest between the two men.

When the banner was in place, Bryan stepped back. "It looks good," he said. "Thanks for your help, everybody."

Max hopped down from the trailer and clapped Bryan on the shoulder. "We'll see you Saturday morning," he said. "Just say a prayer it doesn't snow. I don't want to freeze off any valuable parts while I'm running around up there in my underwear."

"I've ordered good weather, just for you," Bryan said.

They exchanged goodbyes, and Angela gathered her things and prepared to leave. "Angela!" Bryan called as she turned away. He hurried to her side. "Are you leaving already?"

"I have some things I need to finish up at the shop," she said. A lame excuse, even to her ears.

"I thought maybe we could go have a drink somewhere."

"That's a great idea, but can I take a rain check?"

The fine lines at the corners of his eyes deepened. "Meet me after the parade Saturday, then. You'll have time before you have to be at the theater."

"That's a little early for a drink." The Flauschink parade started at three in the afternoon.

"We can have coffee. We need to talk."

She nodded. Yes. They needed to talk. Maybe between now and Saturday she could figure out what it was she wanted to say to him. "All right," she said. "It's a date." *An unfortunate choice of words,* she thought as soon as they were out of her mouth. She didn't want to imply that she and Bryan were dating or were a couple. As long as they were only casual friends who sometimes got together to do things, she could persuade herself her heart wasn't in any real danger.

Right. And Crested Butte's snow wasn't deep and chocolate wasn't good and the world was flat as a pancake.

Chapter Eight

After days of Zephyr's relentless ragging on him to attend the Flauschink polka ball, Bryan finally gave in and agreed to go. It wasn't as if he had anything else to do on a Friday night; Angela was babysitting, and so far she'd refused to go out with him anyway. He had their coffee "date" after the parade to look forward to. That was probably his last chance to persuade her that the two of them would make a good couple.

"Dude, over here!" Zephyr, looking more like a polar bear with mange than a fierce abominable snowman, hailed Bryan as he threaded his way through the crowd at the Eldo Bar. Loud polka music emanated from the rear stage where a band played. Bryan pushed past a six-foot pink rabbit and a cowled Grim Reaper and made his way to the table where Trish and Zephyr sat with Max, Casey, Hagan and Maddie Ansdar and an assortment of single friends.

"Great costume," Maddie said, admiring Bryan's black-and-white striped prison garb. He'd painted the stripes on faded-out khakis and an old sweatshirt, and added a plastic ball and chain from a novelty shop near the college in Gunnison.

"It's perfect," Zephyr said. "Kind of a statement on your real life—a prisoner of capitalism, chained to your desk."

Trish elbowed him. Bryan ignored the dig, though Zephyr's criticisms of his new lifestyle were getting old. Zephyr seemed to think this was a phase Bryan was going through, that he'd soon come to his senses and return to his carefree, slacker ways. That wasn't going to happen and soon enough his friend would realize it—if they could manage to stay friends.

"I see you're giving everybody a preview of our float tomorrow," Bryan said to Max, who was dressed in a pair of bright red, drop-seat long-handle underwear with colorful polka-dot and striped patches sewn on the backside and knees. Red-and-white socks pulled to his knees, sheepskin slippers and a three-foot-long striped stocking cap completed the outfit. "You look like a giant candy cane," Bryan added.

Zephyr made a face. "Ooh, dude, you've put me off peppermint forever."

Casey laughed. She wore a long quilted robe, a frilly cap and fuzzy pink slippers. "I don't think even Carl would object to that outfit as risqué," Bryan said.

"You can't even tell there is a woman under there," Hagan said, his Norwegian accent still evident after years in the United States.

Casey smiled sweetly, but said nothing.

"How's the job going?" Casey asked. "Has the hotel been busy?"

"Pretty busy. I'm learning a lot. My first review comes up next month and I'm hoping for a raise."

"Then you can buy the next round," Zephyr said.

The hotel receptionist, Rachel, dressed as a Playboy bunny, complete with black fishnet hose, rabbit ears and a round, puffy tail, slinked over to their table. "Hey, Bryan," she said. "Wanna dance with me?"

"Thanks, but I just got here." He reached for the pitcher of beer that sat at the center of the table and filled a cup. "I want to visit with folks for a while."

"I'll dance with you, Rachel." Eric Sepulveda, a local paramedic and ski patroller, stood at the other end of the table.

"I'd love to, darling." Rachel gave Bryan one last flirtatious look, then left with Eric.

Bryan sipped his beer, but soon became aware of an uncomfortable silence around him. He looked up and found everyone staring at him. "What?" he asked.

"Since when do you turn down a dance with a good-looking chick?" Zephyr asked.

"Maybe he doesn't want to dance with Rachel because they work together," Casey said. "Some businesses have policies about that."

"Stupid policy," Zephyr muttered.

"It's not that," Bryan said. "I'm just not interested in her."

"Who *are* you interested in?" Trish asked. "Or don't you want to say?"

Bryan looked away. He wasn't about to confess his attraction to Angela in front of all his friends—not until he knew where things were going between them. Despite the amazing kisses they'd shared, she hadn't been overly encouraging so far.

"Bryan thinks he's ready to settle down," Zephyr said. "He's looking for Ms. Right."

Bryan glared at his friend, who grinned back.

"What about Angela Krizova?" Trish asked.

Bryan almost choked on his beer. "What about her?"

"The two of you seem to get along well together," Trish

said. "She's attractive, with her own successful business and you're about the same age. I could see you two together."

"Bryan and Angela?" Zephyr shook his head. "No way."

"Why not?" Bryan asked. "What's wrong with her?"

"She's not your type, dude."

Trish scowled at her boyfriend. "If you say it's because she's fat, you're going to be sleeping on the sofa."

"Come on," Zephyr said. "She *is* a hefty girl. And Bryan here always dates the hottest chick in the room. It's like, evolutionary destiny or something."

"Evolutionary destiny?" Maddie asked. They all stared at Zephyr.

"Sure. You know—the best-looking males and females get together to make the best-looking babies."

"Then how do you explain Billy Joel and Christie Brinkley?" Casey asked. "Or Rick Ocasek and Paulina Porizkova? Or Mick Jagger and Jerri Hall?"

"Rock stars don't count." Zephyr smoothed the lapels of his jacket. "Women can't resist our sex appeal."

"Money might have something to do with it, too," Maddie said.

"Guess I'm breaking all the rules," Trish murmured.

"I think Angela's a good-looking woman," Bryan said. "She's smart and has a good sense of humor, too."

"Then why don't you ask her out?" Casey asked.

Bryan hesitated, then sighed. He might as well confess now—secrets didn't last long in a small town. "I did," he said. "She turned me down."

"You're kidding." Trish's eyes widened. "Why?"

He shrugged. "I don't think she thought I was serious about wanting to date her."

"She's crazy," Casey said. "You're a great catch, especially now that you have a good job."

"So, you only married me for my money." Max grinned at her.

"I married you for love," Casey said. "But the money made you easier to love."

"I don't think Angela cares about Bryan's salary," Trish said. "I'll bet she's just shy. Or she wants to make sure you're serious."

"You mean she's playing hard to get?" he asked.

"No. I don't think she's playing a game," Trish said. "She probably wants to be sure you're really interested. She needs a little pursuing to prove you really want to be with her."

"Bryan's never had to pursue a woman," Max said. "They're usually after him."

"This will be good for you," Trish said. "It'll give you an idea of what it feels like to be the one doing the chasing."

He nodded. He'd been so hurt by Angela's seeming rejection of him that he hadn't considered things from her point of view. It was conceivable she thought he'd asked her out only to add to his collection of conquests.

The band swung into a polka and Zephyr jumped up. "C'mon, Trish, let's dance."

Max and Casey and Hagan and Maddie joined them, leaving Bryan alone at his end of the table. All around him, happy couples laughed and talked and danced, fueled by alcohol and the general atmosphere of freedom and fun that was Flauschink. Not that long ago, he would have been in the thick of things, living up to the costume he'd once worn that had declared him the life of the party. When had that life stopped being so much fun? Was it merely a matter of growing up and moving on, or was he responding to something deeper—an emptiness in his life, and in his heart, that another party couldn't fill?

Angela wasn't merely someone to pass the time with until someone more interesting came along. He didn't want to defeat her or collect her. He only wanted to be with her. If he had to work harder to convince her of that, so be it. Some things—like his dream of owning his own hotel or building a new kind of life for himself or Angela—were worth a little hard work.

As PROMISED, Saturday morning dawned sunny and clear. At two-thirty, the parade floats began lining up. Angela, dressed in her dumpy tweed suit and gray wig for the role of Lillian Troy, left Tanya at the Mountain Theatre float to check on Bryan and the others at the entry they'd dubbed Long Winter's Nap. "How's it going?" she asked Bryan. He and Max were adding more staples to the banner, one end of which had come unfastened during a windy night.

"It's going to be great, I think. Casey and Max are ready."

Angela waved to the couple on the float. Max stood beside the bed, adjusting his stocking cap. Casey was in the bed, the covers pulled to her chin. "What are you doing in bed?" Angela asked.

"I'm cold," Casey said. "This nightgown is a little drafty."

"Don't worry." Max grinned. "You'll warm up when I start chasing you around."

Casey stuck her tongue out at her husband, and the tender look that passed between them made Angela's heart turn over. Jealousy, as green and hard as emeralds, lanced through her. This was what she wanted—the kind of love that went as deep as bedrock, making every darkness lighter and every happiness greater.

"You okay?" Bryan touched her arm.

"What?" She blinked at him. "Sure. I'm fine."

"You spaced out there for a minute."

"I have a lot on my mind, I guess. I'd better get back to my float. This looks great."

"See you after the parade," he said.

"After?"

"Our coffee date."

She hadn't really forgotten, just momentarily put it from her mind. "Yeah, sure. I'll meet you at Trish's place, okay?"

"Great." His smile was so bright, she was still a little blinded as she made her way back to the theater float.

The parade entrants were ordered to line up. Angela's group ended up right behind the Long Winter's Nap bunch. As the floats made the turn onto Elk Avenue, Casey jumped out from under the covers to reveal a lacy, ruffled peignoir set in bright red. Red-feather–trimmed high-heeled mules peeked from beneath the billows of scarlet silk as Max, an exaggerated leer on his face, began to pursue her around the bed.

The little charade was greeted with loud laughter from the crowd. "It's the Red Lady," a spectator shouted.

Angela applauded with the rest at this play on the familiar name for the iconic peak that loomed over town. The Red Lady was a mountain, but also a character that had come to represent the community. Incorporating her into their skit for the hotel was a stroke of genius on Casey's part.

Down the street the floats rolled, to the strains of the high school marching band, recorded music from boom boxes strapped to floats and a serenade by the polka band. Angela and Tanya tossed candy from their float, while Austin and Alex urged everyone to attend the final performance of *I Hate Hamlet* that evening at the Mallardi Cabaret.

Angela spotted a number of familiar faces among the tourists who lined the parade route: Hagan was there with Maddie; Tanya's parents and her brother, Ian, had staked out a prime spot in front of the post office. Couples and families watched and waved, enjoying the parade and being together.

"Is this almost over?" Tanya asked out of the side of her mouth as they neared the end of the street.

"We have to turn around and go back the way we came," Angela said. "Why? Aren't you having fun?"

"I feel ridiculous, up here on display," Tanya said. "Waving and grinning like an idiot."

"But you're on display every night at the theater," Angela said.

"But I'm playing a role there. This is me making a fool of myself in front of all my neighbors and friends."

"You're not making a fool of yourself."

"Guess I'm not as brave as you are."

The float lurched, and Angela had to grab hold of a side railing to keep from falling. As they turned around and prepared to head back up the street, she thought about Tanya's assessment of her. Frankly, she did usually think of herself as brave, or at least not easily intimidated. She was a strong woman who went after what she wanted, whether it was opening her own business or landing a part in a play.

So why was she behaving so differently with Bryan? Why was she letting fear get the best of her?

The floats made their second pass, where they were greeted by the crowd almost as enthusiastically as they had been the first time. The king and queen waved regally from the backseat of a red convertible, followed by a float featuring the Has Beens—past kings and queens in their homemade robes and crowns.

"Are you coming to the theater?" Tanya asked as she and Angela climbed off their float.

"Later," Angela said. "Right now I have to meet someone." She hurried away before Tanya could question her further.

She made it to Trish's coffee shop before Trish or Bryan had arrived. Trish's helper, Kristen, was behind the counter. "Can I use your ladies' room?" Angela asked.

"Sure." Kristen nodded toward the curtain that led to the back room.

In the restroom, Angela changed out of her costume into jeans and a shirt. She fluffed her hair, slicked on bright pink lipstick and studied her reflection. Not great, but at least she didn't look like an old lady anymore.

She stuffed the costume in a bag and returned to the front of the store in time to greet Trish, Zephyr and Bryan. "The float was a big hit," she said. "I bet you win first prize." The local newspaper awarded blue ribbons to floats in various categories, including those presented by businesses.

"Have you talked to Mr. Phelps yet?" Trish asked Bryan. "Did he think it was too risqué?"

"Who cares if he did?" Bryan asked. "It was a great float. I heard a lot of people talking about it." He sat at the table with Angela. "What can I get you?"

"A chocolate chai," she said.

"As long as you're buying, I'll have a large mocha." Zephyr sat in the chair on Angela's other side.

Bryan gave his friend a pointed look. "Don't you have somewhere else you need to be?" he asked.

"Nope." Zephyr leaned back. "Though I was thinking

about checking the snow over on the North Face tomorrow. Our last chance before the lifts shut down. You free?"

"We'll talk about it later." Bryan looked at Angela. "I'm kind of busy right now."

Trish came out from around the counter and took hold of Zephyr's arm. "Come on," she said. "Haven't you heard three's a crowd?"

"Sure I've heard it. What does it have to do with…" His eyes widened and he looked from Angela to Bryan and back to Angela. "Oh, I get it," he said. "This is a *date*. Sorry to intrude, bro." Grinning, he backed away, watching them until Trish pulled him out of sight behind the curtain that separated the front of the store from the back rooms.

Angela shifted nervously in her chair. So much for keeping things low-key. "Don't mind him," Bryan said. "Zeph always has to play the clown."

"It's okay." She forced her shoulders to relax and accepted her cup of tea from Kristen. "He is funny. And he and Trish make a cute couple."

"An odd couple, you mean." He sipped his coffee. "But I think they really care about each other."

"I think they do, too. And that's what matters, right?"

"Right."

They both fell silent, only the tick of a wall clock and the hum of the refrigerator disturbing the peace. Angela wondered if Bryan was thinking of them as another odd couple. Or did he have something else on his mind?

"When are you leaving for Broomfield?" he asked.

"Monday. As soon as I can get away."

"Are you looking forward to the trip?"

"Yes, and no." She peered into her cup, as if the right words to explain her ambivalence were written there. "I always look forward to seeing my mom, and I anticipate all the wonderful times we'll have, shopping and going to the movies and doing the whole mother-daughter bonding thing. And then I get to her house, and reality is never as rosy as my daydreams."

"I know what you mean," he said. "I go home for Thanksgiving every year. It's the traditional big family gathering, and it's a lot of fun. But about noon on the third day, I'm ready to puncture my own eardrums if I have to listen to Aunt Matilda tell her bunion operation story one more time, or endure another of my dad's What's-Wrong-With-Young-People-Today lectures. My mother treats me like I'm ten years old, and my sister and I squabble over the same things we did as kids." He smiled. "I guess there's some comfort in knowing things never change, but by Sunday morning, I'm really ready to come back to Crested Butte. This place feels more like home now than the house I grew up in."

She nodded. "And people here really are like a family," she said. "A sometimes strange, non-traditional family."

"Complete with eccentric relatives, like Zephyr."

"And interesting people you'd like to get to know better." Their eyes met and this time she didn't shy away from the warmth she saw there, but added her own heat. "I've been thinking," she said.

"About us?" he asked.

She nodded. "Would you like to come to dinner at my place?"

He didn't hesitate. "Yes. When?"

"Tomorrow night? The play closes tonight, so I'll have the evening free."

"I'd like that." He reached over and squeezed her hand. "I'd like that a lot."

She took a long sip of tea, hoping to wash down the sudden knot in her chest. It was only dinner. Nothing more. But she and Bryan both knew it was a lot more. Here was her chance to start something with a great guy. Or at least to find out what he really wanted from her.

THAT EVENING, before the final performance of *I Hate Hamlet,* Angela was a nervous wreck, as jittery as if she'd been living on espresso and chocolate. But it wasn't worry about the play that distracted her; all she could think of was Bryan and their impending dinner date. Tanya finally pulled her aside during rehearsals. "What is wrong with you?" she asked. "You're in another world today."

"Bryan kissed me last week." She hadn't meant to say the words out loud, but she couldn't hold them back. She had to confide in someone. Maybe talking with Tanya would help her sort out her feelings, which alternately soared and sank, as if she were strapped in the car of a crazy carnival ride.

"And?" Tanya asked.

"And what? He kissed me. Twice, actually."

"You'll have to do better than that. I want details. *Where* did he kiss you?"

"On the mouth. What—do you think I'd get so flustered over a buss on the cheek?"

Tanya shook her head. "Where were you when he kissed you? With a bunch of other people?" She lowered her voice. "Or were you in a dark, secluded corner?"

"The first time was at Austin's party, but we were alone." The moment had passed so quickly; only later had she realized how on edge she'd been all evening, anticipating it.

"And the second time?" Tanya prompted.

"The second time was in my car." Heat flooded her cheeks at the memory of their passionate grappling in the awkward confines of the front seat.

"*And?*" Tanya asked.

Angela twisted her hands together and shook her head.

"What are you doing, auditioning for Lady Macbeth?" Tanya nudged her. "If you don't want to tell me anything, just say so, but don't tease me."

"I don't know what to say," Angela said. "He kissed me and he told me he wants to see me again, but I don't know what it means."

"It means he wants to see you again. Don't be such a ninny. It's not like you."

She took a deep breath. "You're right. I'm being silly. I don't have anything to worry about." She forced a smile that she hoped conveyed more confidence than she felt. "He's coming to dinner at my place tomorrow night."

"That's wonderful!" Tanya squeezed her arm. "Good for you."

Angela let the smile slip. "Please give me some advice," she said. "I'm not sure I know how to do this."

"Of course you do. You've dated before."

"It's been awhile." Longer than she wanted to admit.

"Only because you turn everybody down," Tanya said. "I know for a fact Jerry Rydell asked you out the first week I was here."

"Jerry asks everyone out. If a woman with no teeth and crossed eyes moved to town, Jerry would be on her doorstep asking for a date within a week."

"But he's not the only one who's asked you. I've seen the way men look at you. Don't tell me you don't notice."

"I know how they look at me. They're wondering if I'd crush them if we went to bed together."

"Don't be ridiculous."

"This whole situation is ridiculous."

"No, it's not." Tanya shoved her again. "A good-looking, gainfully employed, sober man who doesn't have a criminal record, an ex-wife or kids, is crazy about you. What else are you holding out for?"

"Isn't there such a thing as too good to be true?" Angela asked, wincing at the pleading note in her voice.

"Not this time. Just…go for it. Stop being a ninny."

Angela drew herself up straighter. "I'm not being a ninny."

"Yes, you are. Now, tell me what you're going to feed him."

"I have this really good shrimp in peanut sauce recipe," she said. "I was thinking about that, with pasta and a salad."

"And for dessert?"

"I was thinking a chocolate torte. You can't go wrong with that, right?"

"No, I meant the *dessert* after the dessert. Are you going to sleep with him?"

"Tanya!"

"You have to think about these things, be prepared. You don't want to let the heat of the moment overtake you. If the answer is no, you have to think of the right way to tell him that. If the answer is yes, you have to shave your legs, put clean sheets on the bed and make sure you have protection."

Angela put a hand over her eyes. "If I walk into the City Market and buy a box of condoms, the whole town will know by nightfall."

"So, drive to Gunnison. Just don't take any chances on being caught unprepared."

Angela took a deep breath. "You're right. I'm being silly. I'm going to focus on enjoying a wonderful evening and not worry about the future."

"Great. In the meantime, we have a play to perform. Can you pull it together enough to try the scene again?"

"Yes. And thanks for talking me off the ledge."

"What's a director and a best friend for? But don't call me Sunday night. You're on your own then. I know you've got good instincts, so use them."

Chapter Nine

As Bryan dressed for his dinner with Angela, he tried to tell himself this was a date like hundreds of others he'd had. Dinner with a woman who interested him.

But everything with Angela felt different. More…significant. Angela represented new territory—a woman he wanted who he wasn't sure wanted him. He'd be lying if he said his ego hadn't been a little bruised by her reluctance to respond to his advances. But more than his vanity was on the line here. He wanted Angela to see him as the man he was trying to be—mature, responsible, with big plans for the future.

Plans he was sure could include her—if she'd let him be a part of her life.

He knocked on her door promptly at seven o'clock and struggled not to fidget while he waited for her to answer. He had raised his fist to knock again when the door swung open. He had the impression of a fall of shining dark hair, deep blue silk in soft folds around her, and the subtle scent of roses and cinnamon. Then their eyes met and he forgot everything else in the warm welcome he found there.

"Come in," she said, and held the door open wider.

"You look great," he said, as he followed her through the

front room into a large open space filled with an antique oak table and chairs.

"Thank you." She smiled over her shoulder at him. "You look very nice yourself, but then, you always do."

"You only think that because you haven't known me very long," he said. "You should see me after a softball game. You won't want to come near me then."

"Hmmm." She walked to a sideboard and picked up a bottle of wine. "Would you like something to drink?"

"Let me open that," he said, taking the bottle and corkscrew from her.

"All right." She stepped back and watched as he twisted the opener into the cork.

He could feel her gaze on him as he struggled to free the cork, her silence unnerving. "How did the performance go last night?" he asked.

"It went well, I think. One of our better-attended performances."

"That's great." He yanked the cork free and poured wine into two glasses. "I wish I could have seen the play again," he said, handing her a glass. "I was so busy watching you the first time, I didn't pay much attention to the story."

He felt absurdly gratified by the pink blush that rose to her cheeks. "Shame on you," she said, her eyes sparkling. "You'd better not let Tanya hear that."

"I won't be the one to tell her." He winked, and her cheeks flushed hotter still. This was a side to the serious Ms. Krizova he hadn't seen before—a softer, more vulnerable side that bolstered his own confidence.

"Are you hungry?" she asked.

"I'm hungry for a lot of things," he said, his gaze locked

to hers. He reasoned he might as well go for broke tonight. She might end up kicking him out, but one way or another, before the evening ended he'd know how she really felt about him.

She turned away. "I hope you're not allergic to shrimp or peanuts," she said, starting toward the kitchen.

Even if he had been, he probably would have risked breaking out in hives before he said anything. "I love shrimp *and* peanuts," he said. He followed her into the cramped space where an old-fashioned gas stove and newer side-by-side refrigerator were crowded alongside a small butcher-block-topped counter. "What can I do to help?"

"Nothing, really. It's a tight fit in here." She opened the refrigerator and stepped back as he moved forward. They collided, her soft backside against his thighs.

He acted on pure instinct, his arms going around her, the heat of her skin seeping through the cool silk. He leaned forward, inhaling deeply. "I like your perfume," he said. "Very sexy."

She whirled around so quickly she almost hit him in the nose. "Why don't you go wait in the dining room?" she said. "I'll bring the food right out."

He smiled. If nothing else, her uncharacteristic nervousness showed he had *some* effect on her. He retreated to the dining room and moments later she appeared with two salad plates.

They sat across from each other. She kept her gaze firmly on her plate; he watched her. Her hair was a rich caramel color. He remembered how soft it had been when he'd twined his fingers in it as they kissed.

"Will you stop that," she said, looking up from her plate.

"Stop what?"

"Stop staring at me. Haven't you seen a woman eat before? Or do all those skinny things you usually go out with only pick at their food?"

"Now you stop it," he said.

"Stop what?" Her expression held a challenge.

"I don't give a damn how much you weigh or don't weigh, or eat or don't eat." His expression was as hard as her own. "You're only using those things as an excuse to keep me at a distance."

Her mouth tightened, and she stabbed at her salad so hard a piece of lettuce jumped off the plate. "Eat your salad," she said. "I don't want the entrée to get cold."

He ate, doing his best not to stare at her, though he was aware of her every movement. Let her think about what he'd said; given enough time, maybe the truth of it would soak in.

"OF ALL THE RIDICULOUS, arrogant, insulting things to say." Angela muttered to herself as she scraped the remains of their salads into the trash. She set the empty plates in the sink. "Who does he think he is, psychoanalyzing me? What does he know about me and what I'm thinking?"

But if she was honest with herself, she had to admit there was some truth in what Bryan had said. She *was* trying to keep him at a distance. What woman would blame her, considering Angela's previous experience with a smooth-talking, good-looking man. *But Bryan is not Troy,* the voice in her head that insisted on being honest said.

She closed her eyes and leaned against the counter, remembering the feel of his arms around her, his body tight against hers. He'd said before that he wanted her and boy, did she want him. That was one truth she wasn't even going to pretend to deny. But what should she do about it? Did she dare go for broke, invite him to spend the night, consequences be damned?

Or should she protect herself with more than a condom and send him packing—possibly forever?

"Do you need some help in there?"

She started. What was she doing, standing in here day-dreaming? She removed the entrées from the oven, where she'd left them to warm, and carried them into the dining room.

"That smells awesome," he said, standing and relieving her of one of the plates.

"Dig in," she said, and proceeded to do so. So what if it was impossible to look sexy and slurp pasta at the same time? This was one of her favorite dishes and she wasn't going to let some man—no matter how good-looking—keep her from enjoying it.

"This is great," he said. "You'll have to give me the recipe."

She somehow managed to avoid spitting out pasta and peanut sauce and stared at him. "You cook?"

He feigned offense. "Why do you act so surprised? I make a mean Top Ramen."

She laughed. "I didn't have you pegged as a gourmet chef."

"You're right. I'm a lousy cook. But this would be a great dish to serve guests at my inn."

"That's right—your boutique inn. I hadn't forgotten." She twirled pasta around her fork. "But if you hire a chef, he—or she—will have their own recipes."

"Maybe so. But I'll have to see if I can talk you into making all the desserts."

"Then you think your inn will be in Crested Butte?"

"I hope so. I like it here. I want to stay. I came to the area for the snowboarding, but there's a lot more going on here than that. What about you? How did you end up here?"

She'd been looking for a place to start over—someplace far from Troy and his new leading lady. "A friend told me about the town. She'd visited on vacation and she made it sound so nice." She shrugged. "I came to visit, and never left. I got involved in the Mountain Theatre and opened my shop and now I can't imagine living anywhere else. It's a special place."

"With some special people." His eyes met hers and a sudden hot shiver of desire rushed through her, its intensity catching her by surprise.

She shifted her gaze to her plate, which was empty. "I have chocolate torte for dessert," she said.

"Maybe later." She heard the scrape of his chair on the floor, then he was standing beside her, his hand on her shoulder. "Angela."

Three simple syllables. A name she'd heard for twenty-six years. Yet it had never sounded this way before, both a caress and a plea. She felt fixed in place, unable to move or speak or even to breathe.

"You look like you're about to faint," Bryan said. "Please don't do that."

"I'm not going to faint. I'm not the fainting type." She raised her eyes to his and saw that he was smiling. "Now you're teasing me," she said.

"Only because you're so much fun to tease." He slid his hand to her elbow. "Stand up for a minute."

She did as he asked; with his eyes staring into hers and his hand caressing the soft skin at the curve of her arm, she doubted she could have refused him anything.

When they were facing each other, he rested his other hand at her waist. "Shall we dance?" she asked, desperate to break the tension building between them.

He leaned in close, his mouth almost resting against her ear. "I was thinking of a different kind of dance. A different sort of dessert." He shifted to kiss the soft flesh at the side of her neck. She lifted her chin, inviting further liberties.

He didn't hesitate, but nuzzled at the base of her throat, the heat of his caress fanning out along nerve endings she'd forgotten she possessed. "You feel it, don't you?" he said, his mouth still resting against her throat.

"Feel what?"

"This attraction between us. This...desire." He kissed the side of her jaw, his hand tightening on her waist.

"Yes," she whispered. "Yes, I feel it."

"If you want me to stop, you'd better tell me now."

"I don't want you to stop." Wasn't that why she'd invited him here tonight? Because she was tired of holding back and second guessing every emotion. Because she wanted to give her feelings free rein and see where they would lead.

He kissed the corner of her mouth. "Should we move to the bedroom?" he asked.

She pressed her hands against his chest, enlarging the space between them, and took a deep breath. But that didn't succeed in clearing her head, since all she could smell was the soap-and-lime scent of him. "Is something wrong?" he asked, his gaze searching.

"Bryan." She swallowed and began again. "If this is just about a night of fun sex, I'm okay with that. But I'd like to know up front."

His grip on her tightened almost painfully. "Haven't you heard anything I've said? This isn't about sex with me. Or not only about sex. I do want to make love to you, but not only your body." He slid his hands up her body and smoothed back her hair. "I want to love all of you."

Something within her gave way at these words. Whether it was because she truly believed him or because she only wanted to believe him, she didn't care. He'd breached the last flimsy barrier she'd erected. "Then love me," she whispered, and took his hand, and led him to her room.

ANGELA'S ROOM was like the woman herself, a mix of practicality and femininity. A pink-and-yellow quilt covered her brass bed, along with the crowd of pillows in various sizes that women seemed to deem necessary to any decor. The walls were papered with old-fashioned, pink-striped paper, and hung with paintings of Gibson girls with wasp waists and piled-high hair, and posters advertising various theater productions.

Bryan noted these things in passing, in the way he'd take note of any new terrain. His focus was on the woman in front of him, on the sway of blue silk over her hips and the curve of her calf beneath the hem of the dress.

She led him to the bed, then turned and moved into his arms. Her earlier hesitation had vanished, replaced by the proud confidence that had drawn him to her from their first meeting in the lobby of the hotel. "I'm glad you decided to stop being afraid of me," he said, brushing her hair back from her shoulders.

"I was more afraid of myself," she said. "Of how much I wanted you."

The words were like pitch poured on a fire, sending desire roaring through him. He kissed her, hard, feeling his own urgency reflected back to him. She opened her mouth and teased him with her tongue, caressing and flirting with coy skill.

Wrapped in one another's arms, they sat, then lay back on the bed. He blindly swept aside the colony of pillows, leaving only two on which to rest their heads. They were tugging at each other's clothing now, the slipperiness of the silk an impediment as he fumbled about, feeling for a zipper or buttons or some sort of opening.

"Stop or you'll tear something," she said, laughter in her voice as she sat up. "I'll do it." She pulled the dress over her head, revealing a lacy bra and panties in the same shade of blue silk.

Greedily, he shaped his hand to one full breast, squeezing lightly. "Did you have any idea how much these have distracted me every time we're together?" he asked, moving his hand to caress her other breast.

"I might have noticed you staring," she said, a satisfied smile playing at the corners of her mouth. "Men do."

"Mmmmm." He buried his face in her cleavage, nuzzling.

She laughed and pushed him away. "Take your clothes off," she commanded.

"Yes, ma'am." He started to strip off his shirt, then, noticing her eyes following his movements, he deliberately slowed, unfastening one button at a time, his gaze locked to hers. "I like watching you watch me," he said.

"You're definitely worth watching." She pushed the shirt from his shoulders and kissed the hollow at his collarbone.

He abandoned all pretense of leisure and hurriedly finished undressing, sending shirt, pants, underwear and socks sailing across the room. Kneeling before her, he slid his thumbs beneath the straps of her bra, pushing them down and pinning her arms. Then he laid a trail of kisses across the top of each breast, dipping his tongue beneath the satin from time to time to tease at her nipple.

Her breath caught, then released in a slow sigh, a sound of such longing it brought a knot of emotion to his chest, and he had to pause and gather himself, his head resting on her shoulder.

She reached behind her and unhooked the bra, then removed it and the panties as well. She urged him to lie beside her on the bed, then she rolled over to dim, but not turn off, the light. When she faced him once more, he moved into her arms and they began to learn the curves and contours of each other's bodies, exploring with hands and mouths and eyes, allowing the wanting between them to build and simmer.

Everything about her was soft and lush, from the thick silkiness of her hair to the round perfection of her breasts, the soft slope of her stomach and erotic curve of her hips. He learned she was ticklish behind her knees, and that kissing the sensitive crease where her thigh met her torso elicited a sound deep in her throat almost like a purr.

Angela had almost forgotten the thrill of exploring a man's body, reveling in the firmness of the hard muscle of his arms and shoulders and the velvety dusting of hair across his chest. When she ran her tongue across one pebbled nipple, he sucked his breath between his teeth and she wanted to laugh with joy at the knowledge that she was the one who aroused him so.

He started to lay her back against the pillows, but she stopped him. "Do you have a condom?" she asked.

He shook his head and looked away. "I guess I should have."

"It's okay. I have some." She leaned over and slid open

the drawer of the bedside table, revealing half a dozen foil-wrapped packets she'd driven all the way to Gunnison to buy.

"I should have known you'd think of everything." He kissed her forehead, then reached for one of the packets.

She lay back, watching him, anticipation tickling her stomach. When at last he levered himself over her, the heat and tenderness in his eyes brought a sudden sting of tears to her own. "You are so beautiful," he breathed as he eased into her, and she felt equal to any goddess.

They came together with gentle urgency, the usual fumbling of new partners only adding to the sweetness of the moment. He made love to her with all the skill she could have asked for from a lover, and she responded as she was sure she never had before, arching to meet his thrusts, crying out her pleasure and encouraging his own. Her climax was a triumphant release, and when he soon followed her she felt again the heady sense of power that she had been responsible for his pleasure.

They lay in each other's arms afterward, the covers pulled up around them. He stroked the curve of her hip, smiling as if at a secret joke.

"What are you smiling about?" she asked.

"I knew making love to you would be good," he said. "But I hadn't realized how good."

The praise made her heart feel too big for her chest. Unlike Bryan, she had not had a great many lovers—none had made her feel as special and cherished as he did. On the heels of that thought came another: she was in love with Bryan. Forget taking things slowly, moving from friendship to closer friends to special friends and eventually to the big L word. She'd skipped the qualifying rounds and gone straight to the finals. The idea terrified and thrilled her. The trick now would be keeping her feelings to herself until she had a better idea of how Bryan saw her. The last thing she wanted was to scare him off by moving too quickly.

He slid out of her arms with evident reluctance. "I'd better go," he said. "I have to be at work early in the morning."

"And I have to drive to my mom's," she said with a sigh. "I'll miss you."

"I'll miss you, too. But it's only a week." Though it might end up being the longest week of her life.

"Dinner was wonderful." He kissed her, a lingering caress that made her want to drag him back under the covers. "So was dessert," he added, as he slipped out of bed and crossed the room, gathering up his clothing as he went.

She propped up on one elbow and watched, reveling in the sight of his naked body. There was something about a really nicely shaped male backside.

"Didn't your mother ever tell you it wasn't nice to stare?" he said as he pulled on his jeans.

"I was always a bad girl," she said. "I never did listen."

He buttoned his shirt, then moved to the side of the bed. "I've always had a thing for bad girls," he said, bending to kiss her once more.

"Mmm." She was afraid to say more, afraid to destroy this wonderful moment when everything between them seemed right. The real world had a way of stepping in and messing up such fantasies, but she'd hold on to this one as long as she could.

Chapter Ten

The drive from Crested Butte to Broomfield took four and a half hours—plenty of time for Angela to think about Bryan and the amazing night they'd spent together. It had been a long time since she'd been in love, but she recognized the symptoms—the giddy light-headedness, the smile she could never completely erase from her lips and the feeling that she was completely invincible.

That invincibility lasted until a few minutes after Angela reached her mother's house in a new subdivision a few miles off the freeway. "Angela, darling!" Her mother, a trim woman with stylishly cut, short blond hair, opened the door and threw her arms around her daughter. "It's so wonderful to have you home."

"It's great to see you, Mom. You look wonderful." Vicki Krizova looked at least ten years younger than her fifty-five years and her hair, nails and makeup were impeccable.

Vicki stepped back and studied her daughter. "You're looking tired, dear. Is it just from the drive, or is something else going on?"

"I'm fine, Mom. I'm feeling great." Nothing like a night of fantastic sex to make a woman feel on top of the world. She walked past her mom into the house.

"Have you gained a few pounds since I saw you last?" Her mother followed her down the hall toward the spare bedroom Angela always used when she visited. "A friend was telling me about a new diet that's worked wonderfully well for her."

So much for that top-of-the-world feeling. Angela felt as if a cold shadow had blotted out the sun. "No diets, Mom." She set her suitcase on the bed. "Please."

"But you're such a beautiful girl. If you'd only lose twenty or thirty pounds—"

"Of course! Why didn't I think of that? I'll put it on my to-do list for tomorrow."

Vicki frowned. "There's no need to be sarcastic. You know I only want the best for you."

"I know." Angela put a hand to her temple, where a headache was beginning to pound. "I guess I am a little tired." And hungry. Being with her mother always made her stress-eat.

"Come into the living room and I'll fix you a nice cup of tea," her mother said. "I want to hear all about what you've been up to."

And no doubt she'd have plenty of advice for her daughter on how to fix everything Vicki thought was wrong with Angela's life in Crested Butte.

Angela sneaked a glance at her watch. It was three-thirty. Too early to call Bryan. Too early to start drinking. Only five days, sixteen hours until she could leave.

It was going to be a long week.

THOUGH THE ELEVATION Hotel was closed for business, Carl had left a long list of things for Bryan and the other employees to see to while he was attending a convention in St. Louis. Minor repairs that had been put off during the resort's busy season were being taken care of, and cleaning crews had been called in to steam clean carpets, drapes and upholstery. All the bedspreads, blankets and other linens were being washed, and the rest of the hotel polished to a high gloss. Clouds of bleach-scented steam billowed from the laundry room when Bryan walked by, and the whir of vacuum cleaners and power drills filled the halls.

At the front desk, Rachel and another clerk, Edwin, had been assigned to clean out all the cubbyholes and drawers and to inventory the office supplies. Other employees were counting linens or bar glasses or liquor bottles.

Bryan's main duty was to supervise all this activity and to troubleshoot any problems that arose. He walked the halls, greeting everyone he passed, enjoying the freedom of not having Carl looking over his shoulder. For this one week, he was in charge, almost as if the Elevation Hotel was his own.

But by the second day of watching everyone else work, he was bored. He sat in his office and stared out at the slopes. Brown swaths of grass looked like patches on the melting snow, and the quiet of the normally bustling hotel was eerie.

He checked his watch. Only ten o'clock. Too early to call Angela. He'd spoken to her briefly the night before, telling her he only wanted to make sure she'd arrived in Broomfield safely. Really, he'd wanted to hear her sexy voice, as smooth and rich as the chocolate glaze in which their fingers had once entwined. He was counting the days until he could see her again—hold her and kiss her and feel her arms around him.

The thought made him even more restless, and he started on yet another tour of the empty hotel. At least walking the halls got him moving and made him feel he was doing something constructive. He could have been in Moab right now, riding his bike on scenic trails or scaling rock cliffs. He could be relaxing on a Mexican beach or trekking in the Canadian

Rockies—all things he'd done on previous mud-season trips. A long week of sitting behind his desk instead, surfing the Net and waiting for problems to surface, wasn't a pleasant prospect.

The halls were even quieter this morning. The carpet shampooers were working on upper floors and the window washers weren't due to arrive until Thursday. The front desk was empty, and the washers and dryers in the laundry room churned away unattended.

Curious, Bryan opened doors and searched storerooms. Had his co-workers walked off the job without telling him, leaving him all alone in the hotel?

He was beginning to feel spooked by the time he descended the stairs to the basement, then he heard muffled laughter. He followed the sound to a storage room, where boxes and crates had been shoved aside to make room for several tables, around which sat most of the hotel employees.

They all looked up as Bryan walked toward them. "Guess we're busted," Edwin said, tossing a handful of playing cards onto the table in front of him.

"Oh, Bryan's okay." Rachel smiled and stood. "Come on in and join the first annual mud-season poker tournament, boss," she said, offering him her chair.

Bryan hesitated, aware of everyone's eyes fixed on him. Did Rachel think he'd sanction their goofing off because of his partying past?

He was supposed to be in charge here, and they were supposed to be working. He could almost hear Carl's voice: *The company is not paying employees to sit around and play poker.*

He searched the faces of those around the table. Some regarded him with suspicion, others with amusement. He stopped when he came to the catering manager, Marco.

He sat back, arms folded across his chest, a smug look on his face.

"Marco, did you finish the kitchen inventory?" Bryan asked.

"It doesn't take that long to count cans of tomatoes and packages of frozen peas."

"But are you finished?"

"As finished as I need to be."

It wasn't the answer Bryan wanted, and Marco knew it, but Bryan let it drop. He moved on to Rachel. She was smiling at him. "What about you, Rachel?" he asked. "Did you finish with the office supplies?"

"If I have to count one more pencil or message pad, I'll scream," she said. She fanned herself with a hand of cards. "That kind of thing is just make-work, to keep us busy while there aren't any customers. None of it's really important."

Several heads nodded in agreement.

"Besides," Rachel continued. "We've got all week to get things done. So why not have some fun while Carl isn't here to frown at us all like a grumpy old man."

If *he* frowned at them, did that make Bryan a grumpy old man? And Rachel was right about the make-work. It wasn't that important, though Carl would expect it to be done by the time he returned. "I'll make a deal with you," he said. "We get all the work done first, then the poker tournament is on. I'll pitch in to help."

"What if we don't like that deal?" Marco asked.

"Then you can spend the rest of your week counting cans of tomatoes and twiddling your thumbs, but *not* playing poker."

He kept his expression stern as they stared at him. Some of them looked uncomfortable, avoiding his gaze or shifting in their seats. Marco looked defiant, while Rachel seemed disappointed. But she was the first to speak. "I guess we might as well get the work out of the way," she said. "Carl will have a fit if he comes back and he doesn't have all those numbers to fill up his reports." She threw down her cards. "But if you see me running out of the building, pulling my hair out, you'll know it's because I couldn't take one more stack of message pads."

One by one, the others set aside their cards and stood, some grumbling under their breaths, but most appearing to accept the compromise well. Marco was the last to rise. He glared at Bryan and started to move past him without speaking, but Bryan stopped him. "Is there much fresh food left over?" he asked.

"Some." Marco regarded him with suspicion. "Why?"

"When you're done counting those cans and boxes, why don't you plan some dishes to use up the fresh stuff? We'll have a party."

"I'll have to use some of the nonperishables as well."

"That's okay. Do whatever you need to make it good."

Marco hesitated, then nodded. "All right. That's a good idea," he added, reluctantly.

With a growing sense of satisfaction, Bryan watched them leave. His first crisis as manager, and he thought he'd handled it well.

He wished Angela had been there to see it. His friends had made it a point to tell her about his partying past, but today she'd have seen that he had really put that behind him. There was a time for work and a time for play, and he knew how to balance both.

FORTUNATELY for Angela, her mother did not spend all her time trying to improve her daughter. The two women did go shopping and visited all of their favorite restaurants. They debated on going to a movie, but couldn't agree on what to see.

Angela met Vicki's latest boyfriend, Al, a handsome retired businessman to whom she'd sold a condo in a pricey neighborhood. Al drove a red sports car and Angela suspected his perfectly styled silver hair was a toupee, but he was good to her mother, so Angela liked him for that.

On Thursday night, Al offered to take the two of them to the Blue Parrot, an Italian restaurant that was one of their favorites. "Isn't the community theater near here?" her mother asked as Al pulled into the parking lot.

"Yes," Angela said. "Just a few blocks away." The players had often come here after rehearsals or performances for a late dinner and drinks.

"Angela is a marvelous actress," Vicki told Al. "She does great comedy and once won an award as best supporting actress in a local theater group."

Angela wondered what had happened to that award—it was probably packed in a box with all the other things she'd left in her mother's storage unit when she moved. Funny—when she'd won the award, she'd been so proud. But it, like everything else associated with her stint with the Broomfield Community Players, had been tainted by her breakup with Troy.

Al entertained them throughout dinner with his exploits as a world traveler, relieving Angela of any responsibility to contribute to the conversation herself. She let her mind wander to thoughts of Bryan. She'd spoken to him earlier that afternoon, and he'd reported that everything was running smoothly. "All the inventories are getting done in record time," he said. "I think Carl will be pleased. If you were here, we could have a celebration of our own," he said.

"Oh? What kind of celebration?"

"Well…I'm in this empty hotel with two hundred and

forty rooms—all freshly cleaned and waiting for guests. You could be my very special guest."

The idea sent a hot thrill through her. "Too bad I'm stuck here instead," she said.

"What are you smiling about?"

Her mother's question startled Angela out of her reverie. "Was I smiling?" she asked, pretending interest in the filet on her plate. "I was thinking about a new recipe I want to try in my shop."

"Most women look that way when they think about sex," Vicki said tartly. "With you, it's food."

"Chocolate is not just any food," Angela said, mostly because she knew it would aggravate her mother. She made it a point to order chocolate mousse for dessert, though Vicki declined anything but a cup of decaf with skim milk.

When they were finished eating, Angela thanked Al for the meal, then excused herself to visit the ladies' room. As she waited for them to join her in the foyer of the restaurant, someone called her name. "Angela? Is that you?"

She knew the voice before she turned around. When she saw Troy, her heart stuttered in its rhythm. He was as handsome as ever, his dark hair a little longer than it had been when she'd seen him last, but his shoulders as broad, his waist as trim. He wore a gray pinstriped suit that fit him perfectly and a blue tie that called attention to the color of his eyes.

Even so, he was not as handsome as Bryan—his mouth was too wide, his smile too false. How could she have ever thought differently?

"Hello, Troy," she said, managing to sound much calmer than she felt.

"You still sound as sexy as ever." To her surprise, he pulled her close and kissed her cheek. "How are you?" he asked.

"I'm good. How are you?"

"I'm great. Hey, there's someone I want you to meet." He turned and addressed a knot of people who were crowding into the doorway. "Kim, come up here. I want to introduce you to someone."

Kim had platinum blond hair, green eyes and a brilliant smile. She moved with a dancer's grace and her size two dress probably had a designer label.

"Kim, this is an old friend, Angela Krizova. She and I used to act together," Troy said. "Angela, this is my fiancée, Kim Moorehead."

The hand Kim offered Angela was manicured and adorned with three gold-and-gemstone rings. A large diamond flashed on her left hand. Angela managed a sickly smile and a weak handshake. So she was merely an *old friend*. Apparently, Troy hadn't told Kim about their engagement. Because he was ashamed of her?

"Nice to meet you," she mumbled.

Then her mother and Al arrived, and she was able to excuse herself.

"That looked like Troy Wakefield back there," her mother said, craning her neck to peer over her shoulder as Angela hurried her toward the car.

"Who's Troy Wakefield?" Al asked.

"Angela was engaged to him for a while, but it didn't work out."

At least her mother hadn't announced that Troy had left her at the altar.

Al looked Angela up and down, as if the news surprised him. "Is that so?"

"Who was that woman he was with?" Vicki asked. "She certainly was pretty."

"That was his fiancée," Angela said, her voice flat. She didn't really care that Troy was engaged. It wasn't as if she wanted him back. But did he have to be so *predictable* and choose a woman who looked like she ought to be modeling lingerie? Someone who looked even a little bit ordinary—a woman whose hair or smile or figure wasn't quite so perfect—wouldn't have been such a blow to Angela's ego.

What would Kim have thought if Angela had just happened to mention that not only had she and Troy *acted* together, but they'd also been *engaged?* What explanation would Troy have for choosing such an unlikely partner?

"Well, I'm sure she isn't nearly as talented as you are." Vicki sniffed.

"Maybe not." Only thinner and firmer and daintier—everything Angela was not. Had he deliberately set out to find someone who was her complete opposite, or was that merely a coincidence?

"Don't frown like that," Vicki said. "It will give you wrinkles." She leaned over the front seat of Al's car and patted her daughter's arm. "One day you'll meet a man who loves you just as you are," she said. "Someone who recognizes your inner beauty—the kind that doesn't fade."

It was the kind of thing mothers were supposed to say. Words meant to offer comfort. But they only made Angela grumpier. Inner beauty was all well and good, but she wanted a man who thought she was gorgeous outside, too.

And maybe she'd found him. Bryan said she was beautiful, and he was certainly a man who should know. She'd reveled in his praise, but part of her had dismissed his words as flattery from a man besotted by lust.

If only she could trust that his words were true. If only she could trust *herself* enough to believe in his praise.

Chapter Eleven

"Excellent job on the parade float." Carl breezed into Bryan's office the Thursday following the hotel's reopening and Carl's return to work. He waved a single sheet of paper over his head. "I've just learned we received first place in the commercial floats category."

"Thank you," Bryan said. "Casey and Max and the other volunteers who helped deserve a lot of credit, too."

"Be sure to thank them for me," Carl said. He sat across from Bryan's desk. "You've been here, what, over four months now?"

"Almost five," Bryan said. Longer than most of his friends had figured he'd last.

"I hope you're enjoying the work," Carl said.

"I do." Most of the time anyway. He'd always figured if something was one hundred percent enjoyable, they wouldn't have called it work. "I'm learning a lot," he added.

Carl nodded, his expression grave. "You did a good job looking after things while I was away. The hotel was spotless and the employees seemed to be in good spirits."

"Thank you." Bryan managed to avoid looking smug. All the inventories and most of the cleaning had been completed by Wednesday morning, at which time he'd announced a big clean-out-the-refrigerator feast and round one of the first Annual Mud Week Poker Tournament. Marco had outdone himself with the food, creating several new dishes they all agreed should be on the catering menu from now on. On Friday, the tournament had been won by a bellman named Curtis Anderson. Bryan had made it to the next to last round, ending up only fifty dollars in the red, and Rachel had declared it the best Mud Week they'd ever had.

"You've done very well," Carl said. "I see a good future for you with the company if you continue on the path you've set for yourself."

Bryan saw no point in mentioning that he had no intention of making a career with the company. This was only an important stop on the way to being his own boss. "Thank you, sir. It means a lot to me to hear that."

"I'd like to see you rewarded for your hard work," Carl said. He slid the sheet of paper across the desk.

Bryan had assumed the paper was the announcement of their winning float entry. Instead, he saw it was an intercompany memo announcing a Local Lodging Providers annual dinner at the Crested Butte Country Club the following Thursday evening. "Management from the various hotels and inns in the area get together at these things to talk shop," Carl said. "I thought you might like to go."

"Yes, sir, I would." What better chance to talk to some of the people who operated the boutique places like the one he wanted to open someday? He'd make valuable contacts who might give him good advice.

"Excellent." Carl reclaimed the paper. "Oh, and you may bring a date, if you like."

"Yes, sir." Angela would enjoy the evening.

Carl sat back in his chair again. "You know," he said, "I've heard a rumor that the manager of our property in Taos is planning to retire next year. That would be a good posting for an ambitious young man."

"Yes, sir." He hadn't given much thought to leaving Crested Butte, though he could see that a transfer might be the quickest way for him to move up. Would Angela even consider moving? Maybe it was too soon to think that way, but now that she was a part of his life, he had a hard time thinking of a future without her in it. If someone had told him six months ago that he would ever feel this way about a woman he'd known such a short time, he would have laughed them out of the room. Bryan Perry was not the kind to fall hard for any woman.

He'd been a different kind of guy then. Now he felt as if everything in his life was coming together—the right job, and the right woman.

"I can see you're giving it serious thought," Carl said. "I like that in a young man. Do you play golf?"

"Not very often," Bryan said. He and Zephyr and their friends usually looked down on the cart-and-clubs set. They preferred more rugged activities like mountain biking and rock climbing.

"I have a regular foursome at the country club, but one of our members will be out of town this weekend," Carl said. "Perhaps you could join us Sunday afternoon."

"I'm really out of practice," Bryan hedged.

"None of us is ready to turn pro," Carl said. "It would be good for you to brush up on your game. You'll meet a lot of important contacts at the club. And you might be surprised how much business is conducted on the links." He rose. "I'll let the club know to expect you and a companion for the dinner on Thursday and golf on Sunday afternoon."

"Thank you, sir."

When he was alone again, Bryan thought about calling Angela and asking her to be his date for the dinner, but decided to wait. Though they'd spent last night together and had arranged to see each other again Friday as well, he was trying hard to rein in his eagerness. She'd been so wary of getting involved with him from the first that he didn't want to risk her thinking he was pressuring her for anything.

After all, he told himself, they had plenty of time. Time to get to know each other. Time for others to accept them as a couple. Time to plan for a future together.

WHEN TANYA had been hired as director of the Mountain Theatre, she'd proposed an ambitious program of six productions a year. The board and theater group members had responded enthusiastically, but the reality of this plan was that as soon as one production closed, it was time to choose, cast and rehearse the next one.

Thus, on a Thursday two weeks after the last performance of *I Hate Hamlet,* the Mountain Theatre members met at the Cabaret to begin work on their next performance. "I've decided we should stage a production of *The Red Lady's Revenge,*" Tanya said as she handed scripts around the table. "It was the winner in a local playwriting competition, and first prize was a production by a local theater company—which would be us."

"I see there are parts for four women and three men," Austin said, flipping through the script.

"It's a comic mystery with a poignant twist at the end," Tanya said. "Lots of fun to perform, and the audience will love it. I think it will really show off the talents of this group."

"I suppose you'll play Roxanne, the Red Lady," Alex said.

"She's described here as the sultry owner of the hotel where most of the action takes place." He grinned. "That sounds like you."

"Angela would be perfect for the part of the town busybody," Daisy said. "That character has some of the best comic lines. Angela could steal the show with a part like that."

"That character does have some good lines," Angela said, paging through the script. She turned to the description of the character. "Marcia is a forty-something, thrice-divorced, chain-smoking bottle blonde with plus-size hips and a super-size mouth. For most of the play, she wears a Hawaiian print muu-muu." She made a face. "Why is it always a muu-muu? I've never known a woman in real life who wore one, but half the fat women who've appeared onstage have worn muu-muus."

"It's an iconic thing," Austin said. "Like detectives in fedoras and villains in westerns in black hats. A kind of visual shorthand to alert the audience to the character's nature."

"I thought that was the actor's job." Angela closed the script. "Sure, I can play her. But can we please do better than a muu-muu?" Since being with Bryan, she wanted more than ever to be as beautiful and elegant as he made her feel. The thought of appearing onstage in a muu-muu, no matter how comic the role, grated.

"Actually, I wanted Angela to play the part of Roxanne," Tanya said. "That role has some really good lines, too."

"You want me to play the female lead?" Angela stared at the director, while murmurs went around the table.

"You're perfect for the role," Tanya said. "You've got the sensuality the part calls for, and you'll be the ideal foil for the leading male character, Steve. He's a handsome, vain hustler for whom everything has always come easy. He almost can't believe it when he's brought to his knees by this woman, who's unlike anyone he's ever met before."

"That sounds like the perfect part for *you*," Angela protested.

"Who's going to play Steve?" Austin asked.

"I thought we'd hold open auditions for the part," Tanya said. "Though I hope you'll audition as well. I want to find someone with the right chemistry with Roxanne."

Austin frowned at Angela. She decided if people really did have visible thought bubbles, Austin's would have said, *What good-looking guy is going to have chemistry with her?*

She wondered if Bryan had ever considered acting. The two of them definitely had chemistry. They'd spent the night together again last night, though he'd had to leave early to be at the hotel by seven. And she was seeing him tomorrow. She was looking forward to spending the *whole* night in his arms, then indulging in morning sex, then a leisurely breakfast, then maybe more sex—

"Angela, did you hear me?"

"What?" She flushed and tried to look interested in whatever Tanya had said.

"I want you to take the script home and prepare to audition for the part of Roxanne. We'll have open auditions as well, for all the parts. Paulette, you're in charge of costuming. Chad, you handle the sets. Remember, we're going for an Old West feel here, something that draws on Crested Butte's history as a mining town. Get together with whoever you need and come up with some plans for me to look at. Any questions?"

There were none, so the meeting adjourned. Angela caught up with Tanya near the exit doors. "Why aren't *you* going to play the part of Roxanne?" she asked. "That femme fatale type is your specialty."

"I don't think it's a good idea for me to star in every production," Tanya said. "Besides, I really believe you'd be better for this part. You can convey the combination of brashness and vulnerability the role requires."

"*You* can convey that, too," Angela said. "And you actually *look* like a sultry, sensuous woman with a mysterious past."

"Sultry and sensuous are not synonyms for skinny," Tanya said. "If anything, it takes a woman with curves to play a role like that. Think Marilyn Monroe, not Calista Flockhart. Besides—" she nudged Angela with her elbow "—I'll bet Bryan thinks you're pretty sultry and sensuous."

Heat rushed to Angela's cheeks. "What makes you say that?"

"I saw his car parked in front of your house Sunday evening *and* last night. And I heard through the grapevine it was there until very early in the morning."

"Don't people in this town have anything better to do than to keep track of who parks where?" Angela asked, her face still flaming.

Tanya laughed. "Nobody means anything by it. It's impossible not to notice stuff like that in a community this small. Think of it like a big family—people here look out for each other." She leaned closer, her tone confidential. "So…is he as good as his reputation?"

Angela couldn't suppress a grin. "Better."

They collapsed against each other, laughing. Tanya hugged her friend. "I'm happy for you both," she said. "I hope he knows how lucky he is."

"Sometimes I want to pinch myself," Angela said. "It just seems too good to be true." Her expression sobered. "But it's early days yet. Anything could happen."

"I hope only good things happen," Tanya said. "Now go

home and study that script. You're going to make a great Red Lady."

"Maybe so." After all, if she could end up with one of the best-looking men in town as her lover, leading lady in her own romantic drama, why not assume a starring role onstage as well?

FRIDAY EVENING, Bryan showed up at Angela's bearing pizza and a six-pack of beer. "The single man's idea of a feast," he said. "I'd invite you over to my place, too, but it's a room in a house with five other people, so it's not exactly private."

"Pizza is fine, and I like having you over here," she said, taking the beer from him and leading the way into the dining room.

As soon as she'd set the six-pack on the table, he pulled her into his arms. "I had a hard time keeping my mind on my work this afternoon," he said. "I kept thinking about you."

"I've been looking forward to seeing you again, too," she said. They kissed for a long time, and he debated suggesting they skip dinner altogether, but his stomach growled and the aroma of pepperoni reminded him he had skipped lunch. He reluctantly pulled out of her arms. "I think the pizza's getting cold."

He opened the beer while she set out plates and napkins, then they sat down to eat. "I've got some good news," he said, sliding a slice of pizza onto his plate.

"Me, too," she said. "You first."

"Our float won first place in the business category of the parade," he said. "I even got an attaboy from Carl."

"Good for you. I guess it wasn't too risqué after all."

"There's more. Apparently, there's an annual dinner at the country club where all the local hotel managers and inn owners get together and talk shop. Carl asked me to come with him."

"That's great. Maybe you'll be able to talk to some of the owners of smaller inns and pick up some ideas for your place."

He grinned. "That's another thing I love about you—we think alike." He used the word *love* casually, testing the waters. Her cheeks flushed a little pinker, but she looked pleased. "Carl said I could bring a date," he added. "I was hoping I could talk you into going with me. It's next Thursday at seven."

"To the country club? I hear the food's really good there."

"So the only thing you care about is a fancy meal?"

"I'm obviously a woman who enjoys her food." She laughed at his look of mock hurt. "Of course, I'd love to go with you."

"Great." He took a long drink of beer and studied her. She had a spot of pizza sauce on her chin. He leaned forward and kissed it away. "What's your good news?"

"The community theater group met last night. We're going to stage a new play and Tanya's asked me to try out for the lead."

"That's terrific," he said. "What's the part?"

"It's a new play, set in Crested Butte. The lead is named Roxanne, known as the Red Lady. She's described as a sultry, sensuous woman with a mysterious past."

"You'll be perfect, you sultry, sensuous, mystery woman you."

"There's nothing mysterious about me," she protested.

"No. The only mystery is that you haven't had a starring role before. Not as gorgeous, sexy and talented as you are." He emphasized each adjective with a kiss, shoving the pizza box aside to pull her closer.

He was considering clearing the table completely and suggesting they make love on top of it when she drew back. "You're certainly in a good mood tonight," she said.

He grinned. "What can I say? You bring out the best in me. Or maybe it's the beast." He leaned forward, but she fended him off again.

"Let's slow down and talk a little bit," she said. "I really can't think straight when you're kissing me that way."

"What do you want to think about?" he asked. He hoped she wasn't having doubts about them again.

She sat back and sipped her beer, studying him. "This is a little ironic, considering we're already sleeping together, but we should get to know each other better. I mean, I know you came here from Texas when you finished college, but I don't know anything about your family. Do you have any brothers or sisters?"

"I have one older sister. She's married with two children—boys. My mom and dad own a sports bar in Dallas. What about you?"

"My parents are divorced. My dad is married to his third wife and lives in Houston. My mom is still single and is in Broomfield, where she works as a real estate agent. I'm an only child."

"And you moved here from Broomfield," he said.

"That's right. Three years ago."

"Because a friend told you about the place, so you came here and fell in love. I remember."

An emotion he couldn't read flashed across her face. "That isn't exactly the *whole* story," she said.

He scooted his chair closer to hers. "Tell me."

She nodded. "I want to tell you. It'll help you understand some things about me. But first, I need another beer."

He opened a fresh beer for each of them, then sat beside her.

"I belonged to the community theater in Broomfield," she

began. "There was a man in the group—Troy. There's a guy like him in every theater company, I guess—the really handsome guy who always plays the leading man. He was the kind of guy who always had women following after him and all his girlfriends looked like models. But he wasn't vain about his looks, and everybody liked him."

Bryan shifted in his chair. She could have been describing him, except for the acting part. "Were you involved with this guy?" he asked.

"I'm getting to that." She took a long drink of beer. "I was in a play with Troy. I played the role of the hero's nutty sister who helps him win the heart of the girl he loves. Troy, of course, was the hero. We spent a lot of time together, learning our lines and hanging out. One thing led to another, and—"

"I get the idea," he said, his stomach twisting with jealousy.

"It wasn't just sex," she said. "At least not for me." Her lower lip trembled, and he had to grip the edge of the chair to keep from pulling her to him. He wanted to tell her he didn't need to hear the rest. Whatever had happened between her and that loser didn't matter to the two of them. But he could see that she needed to get this off her chest, so he made himself sit still and listen.

"I fell in love with him," she said. "And I believed him when he said he loved me. Even though I wasn't the type of woman he usually dated, I thought that didn't matter, that we could make it work."

She fell silent. Bryan waited. He knew there had to be more. Obviously, this guy had hurt her. "What happened?" he prompted.

She took a shaky breath. "He asked me to marry him. I

said yes. I couldn't believe it. I was going to marry this gorgeous, popular, fun guy, who said he loved me. I thought everything was perfect.

"We both agreed we didn't want a big, fancy wedding," she continued. "He bought me a ring and we decided to get married at the courthouse, then go away for a weekend honeymoon. He was already working on another play—a drama I didn't have a part in—and he needed to get back for rehearsals."

"You were engaged?" Bryan tried to wrap his mind around this idea. Angela had intended to marry another man?

She nodded. "The day of the wedding came. I had a girlfriend who was going to be one of the witnesses, so she and I drove to the courthouse together, where Troy and I had agreed to meet. We got there early and didn't think anything of it when he wasn't waiting for us. He had a habit of being late. Even when it was time for the ceremony and he hadn't shown up, I wasn't too worried. I knew he'd get there.

"But then it got to be ten minutes after. Fifteen minutes after. I called his cell phone, but he didn't answer. The judge and my friend were staring at me. When it got to be half an hour after, the judge said we'd have to reschedule and my friend and I left the courthouse. We were walking to the parking lot and I was trying not to cry when my phone rang. It was Troy. He apologized for not calling before, but said he couldn't go through with the wedding. He realized he didn't really love me, he'd just been caught up in the excitement of the play and the moment. The two of us weren't right for each other and he knew I'd understand, and all of that." She squeezed her eyes shut, but not before two tears slipped down her cheeks.

Bryan pulled her close, rocking her in his arms. "I'd do anything to take away that hurt," he murmured, stroking her hair.

She nodded. "I know." She sniffed and straightened to look at him. "You see now why I was so hesitant to get involved with you. In some ways, the two of you have a lot in common."

"You're wrong," he said. "I'd never treat you—or any woman—that way. I really do love you, Angela." His voice caught. He'd never said those words to a woman before, but he'd never meant any words more. "That isn't a line to get you in bed, or something blurted in the heat of the moment. I've never felt this way about any other woman."

"I believe you." Her smile was shaky, but her voice was firm. "But it's hard to trust my own feelings, sometimes. I saw Troy while I was in Broomfield last week."

"Oh?"

"He introduced me to his fiancée—a size-two platinum blonde who probably models lingerie in her spare time."

The pain in her voice made Bryan want to hunt down the jerk and pound him. "He sounds like a walking cliché."

"Yeah, well, he wouldn't be the first guy to prefer gorgeous women."

"Come here." He stood, pulling her with him, then led her into the bedroom, where he undressed her slowly, kissing each inch of exposed flesh, savoring the beautiful package he unwrapped. "I wish you could see yourself the way I see you," he said. "Then you'd know how beautiful you really are."

"You make me feel beautiful," she said, helping him out of his shirt and pants. "Beautiful and sexy, and the luckiest

woman in the world." She pulled him down the bed beside
her. "Can you stay with me all night tonight?" she asked.

"Yes." He kissed the top of her shoulder. "I'm going to stay
and make love to you all night, and in the morning when we
wake, I'll start all over again."

"Then we'd better get started," she said, and leaned over
to dim the light.

Chapter Twelve

Angela awoke the next morning half-afraid the events of the night before had been a dream. She lay still for a long moment, eyes tightly shut, recalling the intensity with which she and Bryan had made love, as if determined to draw as much pleasure as possible from each moment together. Surely the strength of their physical attraction had to be due to more than hormones or pheromones or some other scientific phenomena. Was it possible they felt this way because they were meant to be together? Because they really and truly were in love?

She opened her eyes and studied him as he slept beside her. Thick, dark lashes fringed his eyelids, while the dark shadow along his firm jaw erased any suggestion of femininity. She studied his lips and remembered how tenderly they'd kissed her, how he'd touched her as if marveling at the feel and shape of her.

When Troy had made love to her, he'd never really looked at her. Self-conscious of her body, she'd been grateful for his inattention, content to hide under the cover of darkness, or to take advantage of the camouflage of blankets or clothes. With Bryan, sex was so different—more open and honest, but more challenging, too. The daring, free woman she wanted to be continually clashed with all her old insecurities about her body. She didn't like to look at herself in the mirror, so she had a hard time believing anyone else would enjoy the sight of her nakedness.

She scolded herself for even thinking of Troy with Bryan beside her, but her former fiancé had been on her mind since she'd seen him. She'd spent so many years nursing the hurt and anger of his betrayal, but now she could see he'd done her a favor. What if they had married? What if she'd ended up legally bound to a man with whom she had so little in common—a man who might always be secretly ashamed of her? What misery to be locked in a union with little hope of true happiness.

Instead, Troy had released her from that trap, freeing her to come to Crested Butte, where she'd opened a successful business and made new friends. And now she'd met Bryan—a man similar to Troy in some ways, but so different from him in ways that really counted.

Being careful not to wake him, she slipped from the bed and tiptoed into the bathroom. She almost laughed at the tousled hair and smudged makeup reflected in her mirror. Now there was a sight to make a man think twice about staying the night.

She turned on the shower and stepped under the steamy spray, sighing happily as the hot water cascaded over her. Humming to herself, she washed and rinsed her hair, then turned to let the water run over her face. She'd rate a hot shower second only to great sex on the list of life's pleasures. Well, maybe third. There was, after all, chocolate.

She turned around again and opened her eyes and was startled to see Bryan on the other side of the glass shower door. He stared at her, eyes wide, mouth slightly open, clearly stunned. She instinctively turned to cover herself. With shaking hands, she shut off the water, reminding herself that he had, after all, seen her naked before.

But that had only been in the dimmed lights of the bedroom, in the heat of passion. The bright fluorescent glare of the bathroom lights was not so forgiving, and she was suddenly painfully aware of every bit of excess flesh, every sag and stretch mark, every part of her that was rounded out that should have been curved in.

She opened the shower door and reached past him for a towel. "Excuse me," she mumbled, wrapping the towel around herself. He made no move to speak or stop her as she ran from the room.

So much for the wonderful, perfect relationship. The poor man had probably been horrified at the sight of all that white, naked flesh. No matter how much he professed to love her, the reality of her sheer bulk compared to the other women he had known must have been a shock to his system.

After a moment, she heard the shower resume running, and she took advantage of the opportunity to dress. She towel-dried her hair, then pulled it back in a ponytail. By the time Bryan emerged from the bedroom, she was in the kitchen, making breakfast. "Good morning," he said, and kissed her, but there was no mistaking the sudden awkwardness between them. As they ate, they talked in generalities, and his eyes could not meet hers. And there was no talk of returning to bed, or even of when they would see each other again.

Angela felt as if a giant fist squeezed her heart, and it took every bit of acting ability she possessed to smile and pass the toast and not demand that he tell her—at once—what was wrong. But she was too afraid of what his answer might be.

She was almost relieved when he left. "I promised Zephyr I'd help him with a project over at Trish's," he said, and kissed her goodbye.

She shut the door, then sank into a chair, not even bothering to watch him drive away. "Oh, no," she whispered, in too much pain even to cry.

"DUDE, WHAT IS WRONG with you this morning?" Zephyr asked. He snatched the saw from Bryan's hand. "You just sawed that all crooked. And before that, you almost nailed the door shut."

The two friends were on Trish's back porch, attempting to enclose part of the space to serve as storage. "What's going on?" Zephyr asked. "And don't say nothing. If *I* think you're a space cadet, you know you're way out there."

"I spent the night with Angela last night," Bryan admitted.

Zephyr laid the saw to one side and settled himself against one of the sawhorses they'd set up on the porch. "Tell me something I don't know."

"What do you mean, you knew?"

"Dude, your car is always parked in front of her place these days. I didn't think the two of you were exchanging recipes."

"But you never said anything."

"Who you sleep with is your business, dude." Zephyr grinned. "I'd have never pegged Angela as your type, but if you dig her, she must have more going for her than her chocolates."

"Don't joke around," Bryan said. "This is serious. I think I might be in trouble here."

Zephyr's expression sobered. "What kind of trouble? Is she pregnant?"

"No, she's not pregnant." At least, he hoped she wasn't. "It's not her, it's me."

"*You're* pregnant?" Zephyr's eyebrows rose.

Bryan glared at him. "Will you listen?"

"I'm trying, but you're not making sense. Spit it out, dude. What's wrong?"

"I'm in love." Even saying the words out loud made his heart beat faster.

"Is that all?"

"What do you mean, is that all?" To him, it was everything.

"You don't look very happy about it."

"I am happy. And scared. And confused." He shook his head. "I've never felt this way about anyone before and…and I'm not sure I like it. It feels sort of…out of control."

"That's only because you haven't had much practice yet," Zephyr said. "Once the newness wears off, it'll get better."

"I'm not so sure about that." Bryan had thought he could handle it—thought there wasn't anything in the world better than the way he felt when he was with Angela. She made him feel more confident, more alive, even *smarter* than he did at any other time.

Then this morning, he'd walked in on her while she was taking a shower. The sight of her standing there naked, her head tilted up toward the spray, water streaming down her body, had paralyzed him in his tracks. She was so beautiful; he had realized that every part of her was precious to him.

That awareness hit him hard and strong. In that moment, he knew he would do anything to protect her, anything to keep her from being hurt, anything to make her happy. An injury to her would wound him, and the thought of losing her made him sick and cold inside. She had a power over him he would have never allowed anyone, yet he'd surrendered to her without argument.

"Have you told her you love her?" Zephyr asked.

Bryan nodded.

"And did she say she loved you back?"

"Yes."

"Then what are you worried about? You love each other. I assume the sex is good. Time for happily ever after."

Bryan glared at him. "I can't believe I'm asking you for relationship advice."

"Hey, I happen to be in a very good relationship with a wonderful woman," Zephyr said. He stood. "And she's going to pitch a fit if we don't finish this shed like I promised. So, come on. Get to work."

"Why didn't she hire a carpenter?" Bryan asked, picking up the saw again.

"Because I work for free. Come on."

Bryan forced himself to focus on his work, to forget about Angela for a while. But Zephyr brought the subject up again.

"Maybe your problem isn't really being in love with Angela," he said.

"What makes you say that?"

"Maybe your real problem is that you can't make the feelings in your heart and the thoughts in your head match up."

"Now you're not making sense." Not that that was anything new with Zephyr.

"Think about it. Angela isn't the kind of woman you usually go for. To be blunt, she's no beauty queen. And stop looking at me like I just ate your dog. I'm trying to be honest here."

Bryan took a deep breath and reined in his temper. Maybe Zephyr would get to a point—eventually. "Go on."

"But for whatever reason, you're attracted to her. Physically, emotionally, whatever. Am I right?"

"Yes."

"But you're a pretty logical guy. So, the logical side of you—the one that knows you're a man who doesn't have any trouble getting women, beautiful women, to fall all over you—sees you with a woman like Angela and there's a disconnect."

"You're still not making sense."

"Pay attention. Maybe all these weird feelings you're having about being in love are a form of self-defense. A kind of early warning system trying to get you to pull out of this. Before you wake up one morning and realize you're living with a woman who isn't right for you."

"So you think I'm so shallow I can only be happy with a woman who looks like a model?"

Zephyr shrugged. "Can't fight evolution, man. Survival of the fittest might also be survival of the best looking."

"You're nuts," Bryan said. "Besides, I happen to think Angela is very beautiful."

"I can see her appeal," Zephyr said. "But you gotta admit, being in love is supposed to be a pleasant experience, and you don't look like you're having much fun at all."

"Maybe it's like you said before. I need more time to get used to the idea."

"Well, while you're getting used to it, give me a hand with this panel here." He hefted a section of plywood. "Just remember, there are worse things than being in love."

"Let me guess—not being in love." He helped hold the panel in place while Zephyr fastened it to the frame they had built.

"I was thinking more along the lines of being eaten alive by lions, but I guess not being in love could be worse, too."

"Tell me again why I'm friends with you."

"Easy. Because I'm so smart and entertaining." He waved the hammer in the air. "And because you know I've always got your back."

As declarations went, it didn't exactly inspire confidence, but Bryan felt some of the tension ease from his body. Zephyr did know how to make him laugh. Maybe the best approach to his feelings for Angela was to not spend too much time dissecting them. He'd relax and go with the flow and things would work out the way they were supposed to.

Either that, or he'd go crazy. Considering the turmoil his emotions had been in lately, who was to say love and insanity weren't closely related.

"Max and I are riding Sunday afternoon," Zephyr said. "Want to come?"

"I can't. I got roped into playing golf with Carl and some of his buddies."

"Golf?" Zephyr stared at Bryan as if he'd suddenly sprouted an extra head. "You hate golf."

"Yeah, but I figure I can pretend to like it long enough to make a good impression on some of the movers and shakers in town."

"What do you care about any of them?"

"That's how business works." Bryan picked up the saw and prepared to cut a two-by-four. "The golf course is where most of the big deals go down."

"I never thought I'd see the day you'd be sucking up to a bunch of suits on the golf course," Zephyr said.

"Give me a break," Bryan said. "What if you had the chance to play golf with a big record producer? You'd do it."

Zephyr shook his head. "The Z Man doesn't play golf. But I could show the producer a mountain biking or hiking trail he'd never forget."

"Yeah, well, these guys aren't interested in mountain biking or hiking. If I have to give up a few afternoons to hit a ball around a manicured course, I'll do it. The faster I get promoted and start making the big bucks, the sooner I'll be able to open my own place."

"Just don't forget who your real friends are on your way to the top."

Bryan set aside the saw and glared at Zephyr. "What do you mean by that?"

"I'm just sayin'. Those guys on the golf course aren't the ones you can really count on. If you make the mistake of choosing the movers and shakers over the pals who've been behind you all along, you might find out why they say it's lonely at the top."

"I don't believe this. I bail on one bike ride and I'm a bad friend." He tossed aside the two-by-four and picked up another.

"I'm just sayin'." Zephyr shrugged. "This job is changing you."

"People change. They grow up."

Zephyr ignored the dig. "Grow up, grow old. It doesn't matter to me. Just promise me you won't turn into one of those stressed-out high rollers who's more concerned about what kind of car he's driving than the scenery along the road."

Was that really where Zephyr thought he was headed? "No chance," Bryan said. "Not while I have you around to remind me."

"That's what friends are for." Zephyr picked up the cut two-by-four and examined it. "Crooked again. Trish is going to pitch a fit."

"Better watch it, or people will start calling you henpecked."

Zephyr grinned. "I prefer to think of myself as a kept

man. Besides, I like to let her think she's the competent one in the relationship."

"Dude, she *is* the competent one."

"And I'm the sexy rock star, so I figure it evens out." He balanced the hammer on the end of his finger. "Everything's a trade-off, y'know? I don't pay any attention to Trish's nagging, and she overlooks the fact that my income stream is erratic. We make it work, because we know what's really important."

"And what's really important?" Bryan asked. He expected his friend to make one of his trademark smart comments about brains and beauty or money and sex.

Instead, Zephyr's expression turned serious. "Don't you listen to the radio or look in the bookstore? Love's what's important. It's what all the good songs and most of the books are about, what makes the world go 'round and the sun come up."

"Right." Bryan nodded. Love. One four-letter word that made his heart race and his stomach hurt. Zephyr thought love was the answer, but Bryan wondered if, sometimes at least, love wasn't the problem. If he weren't in love with Angela, maybe he'd be able to think straight and see more clearly where, exactly, the two of them were headed.

By Monday morning when she arrived at work, some of Angela's anxiety had subsided. Bryan had called her Sunday evening and his conversation had given no hint that anything was wrong. They'd made plans for him to pick her up for the hotel management dinner Thursday and they talked about the possibility of going into Gunnison to see a movie that weekend. He'd ended the conversation by telling her he loved her, sounding as sincere as ever.

Obviously, she'd let a combination of an overactive imagination and her long-held insecurities get the best of her Saturday morning. Bryan was a great guy and everything between them was going to be all right. That reminder—and the batch of cream cheese brownies she whipped up Monday afternoon—went a long way toward relieving her fears.

Angela dressed carefully for dinner that Thursday, in a black velvet sheath with a beaded bodice, a fringed silk shawl, and black-and-silver stiletto sandals that made her almost as tall as Bryan. "You look gorgeous," he said, kissing her warmly when he arrived to pick her up, his gaze sweeping over her in a way that proved the compliment was anything but perfunctory.

"You're pretty gorgeous yourself," she said. In a stylish black suit and silver-and-blue tie he might have graced the cover of a fashion magazine. She didn't miss the interested looks he drew from a number of women as they entered the private dining room at the country club that had been set aside for the evening's events, and allowed herself a small smile of satisfaction. *Eat your hearts out, ladies,* she thought. *He's with me.*

Bryan's boss, Carl Phelps, greeted them as they crossed the room. "Hello," he said, shaking Bryan's hand. "I'm glad you could be here tonight."

"Carl, you remember Angela, don't you? She helped with our Flauschink parade float."

"Hello again, Ms. Krizova." Carl's handshake was firm, if a little stiff. "There are some people I'd like you to meet." Phelps took Bryan's arm. "Please excuse us, Ms. Krizova," he said. "We won't be long."

Bryan sent her an apologetic look. Angela was left standing with a smile frozen on her face, feeling awkward. She didn't see a soul she knew. Fine. She'd get a drink and meet some people. Maybe someone here would like to order some custom chocolates for their guests.

She was standing at the bar when Bryan returned to her side. "Sorry about that," he said. "Carl can be a little single-minded at times."

"Did you meet anyone interesting?" she asked.

"The regional vice president is here, along with some marketing people. I'll try not to abandon you like that again."

"That's all right," she said, accepting a glass of wine from the bartender. "I'm a big girl. I can look after myself."

"We're sitting over here." Bryan led her to a table and introduced her to the couple already seated there. "This is Millie and Dan Alderson," he said. "They own the Cottonwood Guest House in Taylor Canyon."

Millie, a fifty-something woman with a mass of silver-blond curls, smiled in welcome. "That is a gorgeous dress," she said.

"Thank you." Angela settled in the chair next to Millie. "Tell me about your inn. Taylor Canyon is such a beautiful area."

Over their salads, the two couples talked about innkeeping, the spring weather and the local passion for softball. When the waiter had cleared their plates and was serving their entrées, Bryan leaned over and whispered to Angela. "I'm glad you're here," he said. "I'd be really nervous around some of these bigwigs if I didn't know you had my back."

"I'm glad you invited me." She squeezed his hand under the table. "I'm enjoying myself, and the food is excellent."

"We make a good team," he said.

"Yes, we do." The idea sent a warm glow through her. She'd been independent for many years and had always prided herself on her strength and self-reliance, but the idea of partnering with someone, offering mutual support and being there to bounce off ideas, held a strong appeal. Being with someone no longer felt like a weakness, but an added strength.

BRYAN LISTENED to Dan Alderson's story of how he and Millie had started their inn, wishing he had paper to take notes. To his right, the manager of the Econo Lodge in Gunnison talked about an e-mail marketing program he'd launched to bring in new guests. To his left, Angela and Millie traded anecdotes of dealing with tourists new to the mountains.

At times in the past few months, he'd questioned his decision to give up the freedom of a stress-free life with no responsibilities. When his days had been devoted to snowboarding and his nights to undemanding jobs, his biggest worry had been how to scrape together enough spare change to buy a pitcher of beer, or stashing his dirty clothes under the bed before he brought a woman home to spend the night. Now he saw everything differently. He had more responsibilities and worries, but the future held so many more possibilities. He worked hard, but he could see the reward that could be his. He'd made the right decision, and that knowledge felt good.

They were finishing dessert when Carl appeared at their table. "Bryan, may I speak with you a moment?" he asked.

Bryan glanced at Angela. "Go on," she said. "Millie's interested in community theater, so she and I have a lot to talk about."

"All right." He excused himself and followed Carl to an alcove near the door.

"Are you enjoying yourself?" Carl asked.

"Yes. Thank you again for inviting me." In addition to the Aldersons, he'd met a man who ran a successful luxury fishing lodge on Blue Mesa Reservoir, and a woman from

Gunnison who worked as a consultant for small innkeepers. His jacket pocket was stuffed full of business cards, and he had a list of contacts who could help him when the time came for him to start his own business.

"What is your relationship with Ms. Krizova?" Carl asked.

Bryan frowned at him. "She and I are dating."

Carl pursed his lips. "Is it serious?"

"I think that's a personal question."

"Of course it is, and I apologize for being so nosy." His smile was ingratiating. "Now, come over here a moment. There's someone I want you to meet."

Reluctantly, Bryan followed his boss to a table near the bar. "Stephanie?" Carl addressed an attractive blonde.

"Yes?" She looked up from her plate, and Bryan tried not to stare. She was stunning, with the kind of face and figure that wouldn't have been out of place advertising beer or selling cars. Instead, she wore a tailored gray suit that managed to emphasize rather than hide her curves.

"Stephanie Reynolds, I'd like you to meet Bryan Perry," Carl said. "Bryan works with me at the Elevation Hotel. Bryan, Stephanie works in the corporate marketing department. She's a former Miss California, but she has brains as well as beauty. She has an MBA from Harvard and is one of our company's rising stars."

"Carl exaggerates." She stood and offered Bryan her hand. "It's nice to meet you, Bryan. Carl has told me a lot about you. He thinks of you as his protégé."

Bryan wasn't sure he wanted to be Carl's protégé. He liked to think he was responsible for his own success—or failure. "It's nice to meet you, Ms. Reynolds."

"Please, call me Stephanie." She indicated the chair beside her. "Sit and tell me more about the Elevation Hotel. I'm relatively new to the company and I'm trying to learn about all our properties. Carl said you'd be happy to fill me in."

Bryan glanced at his boss, who was already backing away.

"Take my seat," Carl said. "I have some other people I need to talk to."

Bryan sat. He didn't see how he could avoid doing so without appearing rude. "What would you like to know?" he asked. "I've been with the company less than a year myself."

"Then you can give me an outsider's perspective on the property." She leaned forward, giving him a view of her deep cleavage, and lightly touched his hand. "Tell me what you feel the property is doing right in its approach to marketing, and where there's room for improvement."

"I don't think I'm really qualified to say."

"Of course you are." She lowered her voice and looked at him through veiled lashes. "You strike me as a strong man and I'm eager to hear your opinions."

Even recognizing her flirtation for what it was, Bryan found himself dazzled. Stephanie was well educated, sophisticated and inarguably gorgeous. She was probably a lot of fun to be with, too, as long as a man recognized she had an ulterior motive for wanting to be with him. Women like Stephanie, who could have any man they wanted, learned early on how to employ both their beauty and their brains to their benefit. He didn't condemn them for it, but there was no point in being naive about it, either.

He wasn't sure why she'd singled him out tonight. Maybe she simply liked his looks, or she bought into all the hype about him Carl had apparently been feeding her. In any case, he was going to disappoint her. He'd tell her what she wanted to know about the hotel, but he'd make it clear he wasn't interested in anything more.

Chapter Thirteen

Angela wasn't sure how long Bryan had been away from their table when she finally excused herself to visit the ladies' room. Carl was obviously determined to monopolize his time, but since the purpose of this dinner was to make professional contacts, she had no objection. Later on, the two of them would compare notes about the evening and maybe share a laugh about Carl's none-too-subtle maneuverings.

She returned to the dining room and searched the crowd for Bryan. At first, she didn't see him, then a group that had been standing in front of her broke up and she spotted him at a table across the room. She started toward him, then froze in mid-stride. He was seated with a very attractive blonde, their heads close together. The woman had one hand on his arm, and was staring earnestly into his eyes. Bryan was so absorbed in the conversation, he didn't appear to notice anything else going on around him.

"Ms. Krizova, can I help you with something?" Carl approached her, his usual ingratiating smile firmly in place.

"Who is that talking with Bryan?" she asked, struggling to sound casual.

Carl glanced at the couple and his smile broadened.

"That's Stephanie Reynolds, one of our very talented marketing people," he said. "Harvard MBA and a former Miss California." He laughed. "The two of them are so good-looking they put the rest of us to shame, I'm afraid."

Angela stared at Bryan and Stephanie, seeing them as others must see them—two incredibly attractive young professionals, perfectly matched and clearly belonging together. Stephanie was exactly the kind of woman people *expected* to see with a man like Bryan. The kind of woman he was used to being with.

She thought of Troy and Kim. Others no doubt looked at them and thought they were the perfect couple. Who would think that about her and Bryan?

She stifled a groan. How many times was she going to have this argument with herself? The man said he loved her—wasn't that enough?

Stephanie laughed at something Bryan said and he smiled back at her. Angela felt sick to her stomach, but not with jealousy. Jealousy she could have handled. Jealousy would have been almost normal in this situation. But no, the blackness that ate at her was closer to despair, the same feeling she'd had when she'd caught him staring at her naked body in the shower. Yes, she loved Bryan, and he said he loved her. But the first beautiful woman who'd come his way and he'd forgotten all about her. "Excuse me, Mr. Phelps," she said. "It was nice talking with you, but I have to go."

When she reached the table, Bryan looked up, clearly startled to see her. So he *had* forgotten all about her while he was talking to Miss California. "I'm sorry to interrupt," she said. "I came to tell you I'm leaving. I'm suddenly not feeling well. I'll call Trish to give me a ride home."

Bryan was on his feet before she'd finished speaking. "What's wrong? Do you need a doctor? I'll take you home."

"Just a virus or something," she said, lying to avoid making a scene. "I'm sure I'll be fine once I lie down." She glanced at Stephanie, who was watching them with avid interest. "Don't worry about me. I don't want to take you away from the rest of the evening."

"I'm done here anyway." Bryan nodded to Stephanie, then took Angela's arm and led her toward the door.

Carl intercepted them on the way out. "Leaving so soon?" he asked.

"Angela isn't feeling well," Bryan said. "Thank you for inviting me."

"Yes, thank you," Angela said.

"I'm sorry you're unwell, Ms. Krizova," Carl said. He turned to Bryan. "Did you have a good visit with Stephanie? Isn't she an amazing woman?"

"Yes," Bryan said, though whether he was agreeing that he'd had a good visit or that Stephanie was amazing—or both—Angela didn't know.

He didn't say anything else until they'd reached his car. He opened the door for Angela, then walked around to the driver's side. "Do you need me to stop anywhere on the way home?" he asked. "The drugstore or anything?"

"No, I'll be all right," she said. She stared out the side window at the lights of houses twinkling among the shadowed hills. "Carl tells me Stephanie is with your company's marketing department," she said.

"Yes." The silence that followed this single syllable felt heavy with unsaid words. "Is this about her?" he asked. "Are you upset because I was talking with her?"

"No!" She faced him. "I'll admit I felt awful, watching you with her, but not because I'm jealous."

He glanced at her, then shifted his gaze back to the road. "Then why did you feel awful?"

"Because I was able to see the two of you as others must see you. She's exactly the sort of woman others would expect to see you with—not someone like me."

"Who cares what other people think?" he said angrily.

"Don't you?" she asked. "Didn't you tell me you'd do whatever was required to get to where you wanted to be? That you cut your hair and changed the way you dressed and put up with all the corporate BS and rules—because in the end you'd have what you always wanted?"

"What does any of that have to do with us?"

"Being with a woman like Stephanie would get you where you want to be faster than being with me," she said.

"I think the woman I choose to be with is irrelevant," he said stiffly.

"Don't think I wasn't aware of the way Carl reacted when you introduced me to him," she said, her frustration with his refusal to acknowledge the truth rising. "He could scarcely hide his shock. And I didn't miss how eager he was to introduce you to Miss California."

"I don't care what Carl thinks."

"But you *do*," she protested. "You have to. He's your boss and he's the one who's going to decide whether or not you get the responsibilities—and the money—you need in order to one day run your own inn."

He pulled into her driveway, and the car jerked to a halt. Switching off the engine, he turned to face her. "Despite what you think, I'm not a total sellout," he said. "I'll do a lot of things for the sake of my job, but I won't let Carl Phelps— or anyone else—dictate what woman I'm with."

"You say that now, but what about a year from now?" She

swallowed a knot of tears, determined to say what needed to be said. As much as she wanted to believe in fantasy and romance, they lived in the real world, where practicality and peer pressure wielded more influence than most people cared to admit. "I don't want to suffer the fallout when you realize *I'm* the one holding you back."

"You're wrong," he said, but his voice held little conviction.

She unbuckled her seat belt and opened the door. "I wish I was," she said. "But I don't think I am. Good night, Bryan. I think maybe it would be better if we didn't see each other anymore. It was wonderful while it lasted but maybe this kind of relationship isn't meant to last."

She climbed out of the car, ears straining to hear him call her back. She prided herself on being a strong woman, but if he came after her, she wasn't sure she'd have the strength to resist.

He didn't call out to her, though, and as she stood on her doorstep she heard the car start up and tires on gravel as he drove away.

She made it all the way to her bedroom before she started crying. She tried to tell herself this wasn't as bad as being left at the altar by Troy. That she'd prepared herself all along for Bryan to eventually leave her. But all the rationalization in the world couldn't lessen the pain in her heart. She'd allowed herself to hope that Bryan was *the one*—the man who would love her for the rest of her life.

She believed he did love her—the feelings between them were real. But love was a fragile, amorphous emotion, up against the tough realities of everyday life. People started out starry-eyed and hopeful, but at some point their vision cleared and demands of simply living picked away at their happiness.

It might be years before she and Bryan reached that point—or it could happen next week. She remembered clearly the beginning of the end for her and Troy, though she hadn't recognized it as such at the time. They'd been engaged a little over a week. The play they'd been in had closed and they were out with friends, celebrating a successful run. Angela had excused herself to go to the ladies' room, and when she'd returned, two of Troy's friends were leaning over him. "I don't understand why you'd choose her when you could have someone who is really hot," one of the men said, his voice raised to be heard above the noise from the dance floor.

"You gotta consider what she's going to look like after a couple of kids," the other man said. "Maybe you think she's sexy now, but what about in a few years? Do you really want to wake up to her every morning for the rest of your life?"

She could see Troy's face clearly from where she was standing, though he hadn't yet noticed her. He looked stunned, and a little sick to his stomach.

By the time she returned to their table, Troy had recovered, and greeted her warmly. Angela had told herself his friends' comments didn't matter. She and Troy loved each other and love helped them see past mere surface attributes, to the important things that lay within a person's soul.

But as she'd waited for him at the courthouse on what was supposed to be their wedding day, that night had come back to her, and she'd known the truth. Troy was a handsome man, accustomed to being with only the most beautiful women. Whatever his feelings for her, they weren't strong enough to overcome that conditioning. The wedding vows talked about for better or worse, in sickness and health, for richer or poorer. But there was no mention of beautiful or plain, thin or fat. People liked to think appearance didn't really matter, but to some people it did.

Bryan was a smart man. A good man. When he'd had time to think things through, he'd see she was right to step out of his way now, before they got in any deeper. After all, if he saw a train wreck headed his way, he knew the only smart thing was to step off the track.

"WONDERFUL DINNER last night, wasn't it?" Carl waylaid Bryan as he tried to slip into his office unnoticed Friday morning.

When Bryan only mumbled in answer, Carl looked at him more closely. Bryan didn't have to see a mirror to know he presented a sorry picture—ashen skin, dark circles under his eyes, shoulders slumped. After leaving Angela, he'd driven aimlessly for the better part of an hour, before returning home to pace the floor most of the night. He was in no mood to deal with Carl's forced chumminess.

"You're looking worse for wear this morning," Carl said. "Just a word to the wise. It's never a good idea to overindulge at a business function. You might end up doing something you'll regret."

"I'll remember that." Bryan tried to push past his boss, but Carl blocked him.

"I noticed you spent quite a bit of time talking with Stephanie Reynolds. She's a remarkable young woman, isn't she? Brilliant, and very easy on the eyes, too."

"Ms. Reynolds is very impressive, but I don't need you to find a girlfriend for me. I already have one." Or had one. He wasn't sure what had come over Angela last night. She'd been fine when they arrived at the club. They'd enjoyed dinner, and she hadn't seemed at all upset when Carl had dragged him away.

Was the problem really that she was jealous of Stephanie and everything she'd said about his ambitions and society's expectations had been a cover-up?

Carl took a step back. "I'm sorry if you thought that," he said. "I wanted to introduce you to Stephanie because I thought the two of you had a lot in common," he said stiffly. "I certainly wasn't trying to meddle in your personal life. And you didn't say there was anything serious between you and Ms. Krizova."

Bryan managed to control his irritation. "I enjoyed meeting everyone last night," he said. "Thank you for inviting me. I have some calls to make now, so please excuse me."

Once in his office, he closed the door and sank into his desk chair. His head ached and his eyes felt as if they'd been sandblasted. He stared at the phone and thought about calling Angela. But what would he say? That she was wrong about him? That he wasn't ambitious? That he hadn't always dated women other men considered downright gorgeous? That he didn't care what his boss thought of him?

The fact that she'd been right about all these things grated. He wasn't as shallow and vain as such an assessment implied. He was honest enough to admit his flaws, but he had plenty of good points, too. Why didn't she think those positive things—his compassion and smarts and work ethic—carried more weight than all the things she saw as impediments to their future happiness?

Most of all, he loved her. Love was supposed to trump everything else. Isn't that what Zephyr had said? People wrote songs about love, fought wars over love and founded religions because of love.

He couldn't think of Zephyr without feeling a pinch of guilt. His best friend's accusation that Bryan was in danger of sacrificing friendship for ambition sat even less well along-side Angela's rejection. Had Bryan really changed that much? All he'd wanted was to improve his life, but others apparently didn't see all the changes as being for the better.

He snatched up the phone and punched in the number for Zephyr's cell phone. "Yo," Zephyr answered.

"Are you and Max still planning on a ride Sunday?" Bryan asked.

"Yeah. We thought we'd try the trails up on Snodgrass Mountain. The snow should be melted enough up there by now."

"Mind if I join you?"

"What about your golf game?"

"I'll get out of it. You were right. That really isn't my scene."

"Sweet! We're meeting around one at the trailhead."

"I'll see you then."

Bryan felt a little better after he hung up. That was one fence mended. Angela would be tougher to approach.

His phone rang, startling him. He snatched up the receiver. "Hello?"

"Hello, Bryan. This is Stephanie Reynolds. How are you this morning?" Her voice was cheerful and strong. He pictured her seated behind a mahogany desk similar to his own, her shapely legs crossed at the knee, her hair done up in a loose bun. Her suit and shoes would have designer labels and people would turn to watch her everywhere she went.

"I'm fine, Stephanie. How are you?"

"Wonderful. I enjoyed talking with you so much last night. I was hoping I could convince you to have dinner with me this weekend. Maybe tomorrow night."

She certainly hadn't wasted any time. He couldn't deny he

was flattered by her interest. "Thank you, but I'll have to pass."

"Is it because you're involved with someone else?"

He opened his mouth to say yes, but stopped himself. Angela had made it pretty clear she thought they should end things.

He rubbed his temple. Going out with someone else so soon after the breakup would be a slap in the face to Angela. Never mind that she'd been the one to instigate it. He wouldn't hurt her that way. "I was involved with someone, and I'm not ready to start anything new right now."

"We don't have to get serious. We could just go out and have some fun."

For too many years, he'd made going out and having fun his main focus in life. "Thanks, but I don't think that would be a good idea."

"Can't blame a girl for trying," she said. "Call me if you change your mind."

They hung up and Bryan slumped in his chair. Was he being a fool for turning down a woman like Stephanie? Dating her would probably get him the right kind of attention within the company. And technically, since Angela had made it clear they shouldn't see each other again, he was free to date anyone he wanted.

He slid down farther in the chair. Too bad the only one he wanted was Angela.

THOUGH IT WAS well into May, the trails above Crested Butte were muddy and still rimmed with snow in places, but Max, Zephyr and Bryan were able to find plenty of passable routes to test their mettle and muscles. They powered up steeps and raced down the grades, trading insults and encouragement, pausing only to gulp down water or admire the view of sun-washed mountains and the town nestled below.

"You've been sitting behind that desk too long," Max said, as Bryan joined him and Zephyr at the top of one trail. Panting and red-faced, Bryan had brought up the rear most of the morning.

"I can still kick your butt on the downhill sections," Bryan wheezed, leaning over the handlebars of his bike. He was surprised at how out of shape he'd gotten in only a few months of sedentary work. All the more reason to be out here today. Straining his muscles and stressing his lungs felt good.

"This is ten times better than riding around a golf course in a little cart," Zephyr said.

"Yeah." Bryan leaned back against the sun-warmed rock face that bordered the trail and inhaled deeply. The scents of wet earth and new greenery filled his head, driving out all the stale air and stale ideas that had preoccupied him at the hotel.

"Golf isn't that bad," Max said. "But I'd think you'd see enough of your boss all week, without wanting to spend more time with him."

"Carl isn't so bad," Bryan said. "He's just a typical corporate drone."

"Yeah, and he's trying to turn you into one." Zephyr brushed at dried mud on his shin.

"I'm only pretending to be a drone until I can save enough money for my own place," Bryan said. "It's not such a bad deal."

"Speaking of bad deals, what's up with you and Angela?" Max asked.

Bryan eyed him warily. "What do you mean, what's up with us?"

"Are you two serious or what?" Zephyr asked. "Is it time

for me to write a new wedding song, or does Max need to tune up his truck so he can move your stuff to her place?"

"Things didn't work out so good with her," Bryan said.

"Bummer," Max said.

"Whoa," Zephyr said. "Back up a minute. Last time I talked to you, everything was all hearts and flowers. What happened?"

Bryan was tempted to dismiss the question with a flippant remark, or simply say he didn't want to talk about it. It was what guys did. But both Max and Zephyr were in committed relationships with women—maybe they knew something he didn't about making things work. "I'm not sure what happened, exactly," he said. "We went to a hotel management dinner at the club on Thursday. Everything was fine when we got there, but by the time we left, she was saying she didn't think we ought to see each other anymore."

"What did you do?" Zephyr asked. "Spill soup on her favorite dress? Hit on some other woman?"

Bryan scowled at him.

"What did Angela say was wrong?" Max asked.

"She said I was too ambitious." He shook his head. "No, what she said was that dating her would get in the way of my ambition. That she wasn't the kind of woman other people expected me to be with, and one day their opinions would get to me and I wouldn't want to be with her, so she was stepping aside now."

"Chick logic," Max said. "It doesn't make sense."

"She's afraid of being hurt," Zephyr said.

The others stared at him. He held up his hands. "I'm only guessing, but you have to figure she's taken some flack because of her size," he said. "Maybe some guy she dated before gave her a hard time about her weight, or she was

passed over for a job because of it. People can be pretty cruel to anybody who's different."

Bryan thought of the man who had left Angela at the altar, of the hurt in her voice and the tears she'd shed when she'd told him the story. Something like that was bound to leave a scar, but hadn't he promised her he wasn't like that guy? "I never said anything about her weight," he said. "It doesn't matter to me."

"Maybe she doesn't know you well enough to be sure of that," Max said.

"Or maybe she thinks you're another corporate drone who'll do anything to get to where you want to be." Zephyr spat on the ground.

"Shut up about my job," Bryan snapped. "Just because I didn't want to spend my whole life as a slacker doesn't mean I've turned into some kind of monster."

Zephyr remained as calm as ever. "Hey, I get that not everyone can handle an independent lifestyle," he said. "But I think you're going overboard in this quest for maturity and respectability."

"Oh, you do, do you?" Bryan faced his friend, hands clenched at his sides.

"You used to be your own man," Zephyr said. "Now I don't even know who you are."

"Putting on a suit and tie didn't make me any different," Bryan said.

"It didn't make you better than everybody else, either."

"Just like not having a job doesn't make you better."

"You're both losers if you're going fight over something like this," Max said. "But if you *are* going to throw punches, you probably ought to pick a wider part of the trail." He nodded to the steep drop-off to his right.

Zephyr shoved his hands in the pockets of his baggy cargo

shorts. "I don't want to fight with you, man. I just miss the way things used to be between us."

"I know." Bryan felt the tension drain out of him. "Sometimes I miss it, too. But that kind of life didn't fit me anymore. I needed to do something—something that would give me a future to look forward to. You do it, too. You've got your band and your TV show. You're always trying new things. This job is my new thing."

Zephyr scratched his head. "I guess I never thought about it that way." He grinned. "I guess everybody doesn't have what it takes to be a rock star and television personality."

"Yeah, well, some of us commoners are getting hungry," Max said. "Let's hit the trail. Nothing like two miles of switchbacks to take your mind off your problems."

"Last one to the bottom buys the beer," Zephyr shouted, and jumped on his bike.

Bryan was next in line, speeding downhill, teeth gritted, gripping the handlebars with white knuckles. He realized how much he'd missed being reckless like this, reveling in the freedom of the moment.

Zephyr was right about some things. Maybe Bryan had been a little too uptight lately. Maybe he was in danger of becoming a by-the-book corporate drone. There had to be a line between following the rules to climb the ladder, and subjugating his whole personality.

The thing was, he had been willing to break the rules when no one was looking over his shoulder. He'd allowed Angela to bring her chocolates to the fund-raising dinner, and he'd given his permission for the poker tournament and even participated in it. The laid-back, fun-loving side of him still existed, but he kept it hidden away when anyone who might disapprove was around.

He skidded around a turn in a spray of gravel, muscles straining, teeth rattling. He wanted the higher-ups at his company to notice him, didn't he? In order to get noticed, people had to stand out. So maybe he should use his differences—the things that made him unlike any other manager they'd hired—to his benefit. He'd start being more daring in his everyday life, relying more on his own instincts than the company rule book. If he took more chances, maybe he'd reap more rewards.

Maybe Carl—and Angela—would see that he was a man who could think and act for himself. A man who wasn't afraid to take chances on the job—or to love a woman other people had underestimated, but whom he never would.

Chapter Fourteen

"What happened to you, woman? You look awful."

So much for Angela thinking she could keep her split with Bryan a secret from Tanya. The director had foolproof relationship radar, and she'd fixed on Angela the moment she'd walked through the side door of the theater Sunday afternoon. But Angela wasn't above trying to bluff her way past the truth. "I didn't feel like dressing up," she said, easing past Tanya and heading toward the stage, where the other actors and actresses were gathering.

Tanya grabbed Angela's arm. She had a surprisingly strong grip for such a little woman. "There are bags under your eyes I could pack my whole wardrobe in. And what is going on with your hair?"

Angela touched the messy knot she'd put up on top of her head. "I was working on a new recipe today and put it up out of the way." She'd been cooking nonstop since Saturday morning. Her counters were covered with cookies and pastries and her freezer was stuffed with casseroles, though this form of therapy had done little to ease her hurt. No need to mention the under-eye circles were from several sleepless nights in a row. Her bed felt too empty now that Bryan was no longer in it.

Tanya continued to frown at her. "Is that a *caftan* you're wearing?" she asked.

Angela looked down at the billowing chiffon tunic she wore over jeans and boots. "A caftan is longer than this," she said. "But I thought we might want to dress the character of Marcia in something like this instead of a hideous muu-muu. It's the same idea, but a little more flattering."

"You're reading for the part of Roxanne, so why do you care what Marcia wears?" Tanya asked.

Angela avoided meeting her friend's gaze. "I was going over the parts last night and I think I'm better suited to play Marcia," she said. "She's the sort of out-there type that I do so well. And she really does have some great lines."

"So does Roxanne. And that role would be a better showcase for your abilities."

Angela fidgeted with the strap of her tote bag and hugged it more tightly to her body. "I really don't think the audience is going to accept me as a leading lady."

"And I think you're a talented enough actress to show them you can definitely carry the lead. When you step onto the stage in that first scene in a figure-hugging red dress and make that speech about the heart and soul of Crested Butte, the audience won't know what hit them."

Angela shook her head. "I know you're always talking about the importance of not getting stale and of surprising the audience, but I don't think people are ready for this." She turned away and started down the hall again.

"Coward," Tanya said.

Angela stopped. "Being practical and sensible is not the same as being afraid," she said.

"Isn't it?" Tanya caught up with her. "I haven't seen Bryan's car at your house lately," she said.

Angela stiffened. "Since when are you keeping tabs?"

Tanya's hand on her arm this time was gentle. "I want to help you," she said. "I hate seeing you miserable like this. What happened? Did the two of you have a fight?"

Angela shook her head. "Not a fight. We decided things weren't working out between us."

"I thought everything was going really well. I'd never seen you so happy."

"Yes, but…I realized we were too different."

"Isn't that what makes a relationship interesting? The different perspectives and talents each partner brings to the match?"

"But Bryan and I want different things. I'm happy and settled in my life, while he's really ambitious and wants so much more."

"There's nothing wrong with ambition. It's what led you to open your chocolate shop, isn't it?"

"What is this? Your day to contradict everything I say?"

Tanya's expression didn't change and she said nothing, forcing Angela to fill the silence.

"Of course there's nothing wrong with ambition," Angela said. But she couldn't bring herself to admit that she feared Bryan's ambition would lead him to places he wouldn't want to take her.

"The last time I saw you, you were over the moon about him," Tanya said. "I can't believe your feelings changed so fast. What happened?"

Angela sighed and leaned against the wall. "If you decide to give up acting, you could probably get a job with the CIA," she said without a trace of anger. "No one could refuse you information for long."

"I only ask because I care," Tanya said.

"I know. What happened is, we went to dinner at the

Crested Butte Country Club Thursday night. It was a meeting of all the hotel owners and management in the area or something like that. Bryan's boss was introducing him to a lot of movers and shakers in the company, but I could tell by the way he looked at me that he couldn't figure out what a stud like Bryan was doing with me."

"Oh, please. What does he care?"

"You don't understand because you've never stood where I stood," Angela said, anger flaring. "You haven't felt the stares, or seen the questions in other people's eyes. Even if they're too polite to ask—and believe me, not all of them are that polite—I know what they're thinking. How did she get so fat? She'd be so pretty if she'd only lose some weight. What does a good-looking guy like that see in her?"

"You're being paranoid," Tanya said. "And you make it sound like you're the size of a whale."

"I'm not skinny and I never will be."

"So what? You're not the disgusting blob you make yourself out to be, either."

"Not to you, because you're my friend. But not everyone feels that way."

"You're right. Most people don't care. They're so caught up in their own lives and their own problems that you'd have to be the size of an eighteen-wheeler before they'd even notice."

Angela flinched. "All I know is that people like Bryan's boss *do* notice the woman a man like Bryan is with. And they expect to see a woman who is at least as attractive and thin as he is. If she's also smart and respected within the business, so much the better."

Tanya shifted her weight to one hip and studied Angela intently. "I get the feeling you have a particular woman in mind when you use that description," she said.

Angela glanced down the hall, but she and Tanya were still alone. She could hear the others onstage, laughing about something. "Bryan's boss introduced him to a woman from their marketing department. A former Miss California *and* a Harvard MBA."

"Isn't that precious," Tanya said snidely. "What does it have to do with you?"

Nothing. Everything. She twisted the strap of the tote bag around her thumb. "You should have seen them together," she said. "They were perfect. Bryan's boss thought so. Everyone did. And I realized they would never think that about the two of us." She held up her hand. "And before you say I shouldn't care what other people think, how can I *not* care? It's the way this world works. We're constantly being measured and judged by others."

Tanya shook her head. "I'm not sure I'm getting this. You saw Bryan with this other woman and realized that other people thought she was more perfect for him than you are and you told him that?"

"Bryan may not see it now, but one day he will. I don't want to be around when he does."

"Angela. Darling. You know I love you, but since when are you able to predict the future?"

"It's happened before. Not just to me, but to other people, too."

Tanya was silent for a moment, then nodded. "I will admit that sometimes, after people have been together for a while, they realize that they aren't really as compatible as they thought. But to break up with a great guy just because that *might* one day happen is nuts."

"Then I guess I'm crazy." Angela started to turn away. She'd hoped Tanya, of all people, would understand the uncertainty and fear that battered her. After all, Tanya had suffered through the nasty breakup of her marriage. She had found the same healing in Crested Butte that Angela had.

Except Angela had discovered those old wounds hadn't really healed. She'd only hidden them as part of her role as the strong, confident woman. When she'd opened her chocolate shop and joined the Mountain Theatre group, she'd congratulated herself on moving on and going after what she wanted in life.

"Angela, wait." Tanya stopped her again. "I'm sorry. I didn't mean to be unsympathetic. Whatever you decide to do, I'm here for you. But promise me one thing."

"That depends on the thing."

"Promise you'll read for the role of Roxanne—for me. Audition, and if I'm wrong, then you can tell me."

Angela hesitated, then nodded. "All right. I'll audition." She'd certainly had plenty of practice lately pretending to be someone she wasn't. She'd played the role of the strong, confident woman to perfection, fooling everyone else, and fooling herself.

BRYAN PLANNED TO STAY out of Carl's way Monday morning. The older man hadn't been terribly pleased when Bryan had canceled their golf date, and Bryan didn't want to start the week with Carl in a bad mood.

But the manager was waiting for him when Bryan walked into his office. "You missed a good golf game yesterday," Carl said.

"You had great weather for it," Bryan agreed. He'd vowed not to apologize for missing something he hadn't wanted to be a part of in the first place.

"You'll have to join us again sometime," Carl said.

"Thanks, but golf isn't really my game. But maybe we can go hiking sometime. I know some great trails."

Carl's eyes widened. "I don't know about that. Hiking might be a little...strenuous."

"It's a great way to get in shape." He carefully avoided looking at his boss's slight paunch.

"Yes, yes. So I hear." Carl frowned at him. "Is that a *bruise* on the side of your face?"

Bryan gingerly touched the tender, purpling area over his right cheekbone. He'd braked too hard on a switchback, tumbled over the handlebars on his bike, and landed face-first on a fist-size rock. "I fell," he said simply. "It'll fade in a day or two."

"Right. About this doctor's convention we have booked for next month—"

The intercom buzzed and Rachel's voice crackled over the speaker. "Mr. Phelps? Could you come to the front desk for a moment, please?"

"What's the trouble now?" Carl asked, shoving himself out of his chair. He headed for the front desk. Curious, Bryan followed.

A red-faced, middle-aged man and an attractive brunette who might have been his wife stood at the front counter. The woman looked relieved, the man annoyed, as Carl came forward to greet them. "I'm Carl Phelps, the manager," he said with a smile. "How can I help you?"

"When we booked our rooms, we were told the rate would be one hundred and fifty-nine dollars a night," the man said. "Now we're being charged fifty dollars a night more. That is unacceptable."

"Let me see here." Carl studied the computer screen. "I see you're in one of our suites," he said. "How was your room?"

"Very nice," the woman said.

"I've stayed in better," the man grumbled.

Carl's expression remained pleasant. "It looks as if you are being charged the correct rate for your suite. The lower rate you quoted is for a regular king room. Perhaps you were confused."

"I'm not an idiot," the man said. "I know what I was quoted. I was told the suite was one-fifty-nine a night."

Carl looked sympathetic. "I'm terribly sorry, but you are being charged the correct rate."

"Of all the—" the man began.

"You're the manager," the woman interrupted. "Can't you make some kind of adjustment?"

"That would be against corporate policy."

"What kind of stupid policy is that?" the man demanded.

Bryan agreed with the man. He stepped forward and touched Carl's arm. "Could I speak with you a moment, Mr. Phelps?" he asked.

Carl followed him into the small office behind the reception desk. "What is it?" he asked, clearly annoyed at the interruption.

"Why not make the rate adjustment?" Bryan asked.

"We don't do rate adjustments when the client is already paying the best rate we offer for a suite."

"But maybe he really was quoted the wrong rate. Or maybe he misunderstood."

"It's against our policy," Carl said stubbornly.

Bryan glanced toward the front desk. The man was still berating Rachel, who looked on the verge of tears. Bryan shook his head and went to her. He glanced at the computer screen, then greeted the man. "I'm sorry for all this trouble, Mr. McCracken," he said. "I'll get this cleared up for you right away." With a few clicks of the mouse, he'd made the required adjustment, and hit the key to print a new invoice. "I apologize for the confusion," he said, handing over the new figures and smiling at Mrs. McCracken. "I've added an additional ten percent discount for all your trouble."

The man looked dumbfounded, but his wife stepped forward to take the new receipt. "Thank you so much," she said. "That was very nice of you."

"I hope you'll stay with us again soon," Bryan said. "We want another chance to show you that at the Elevation Hotel, we pride ourselves on customer service."

"I'm sure we will," she said. "The rooms really are very nice." She took her husband's arm. "We'd better go, dear. We have a long drive ahead of us."

When they were gone, Rachel turned to stare at Bryan. "I can't believe you did that."

"I can't either." Carl had emerged from the office and now stood behind them, his face almost as red as Mr. McCracken's had been. "I could fire you for that kind of insubordination," he said.

"I turned an angry customer into a satisfied one," Bryan said. "Why would you want to fire me for that?"

"You can't adjust rates every time a client demands it. We'd go broke."

"How often does something like this happen? The profit from repeat business will more than make up for the couple hundred dollars we lose with the adjustment. That man and his wife are going to remember what we did and tell their friends. But instead of shouting about how we ripped them off, they'll talk about how nice their room was and how we settled this confusion over their room charges. You can't buy that kind of goodwill."

Carl's face was less red, though he continued to look grumpy. "This is very unorthodox," he said.

"I guess I'm an unorthodox kind of guy."

Carl's eyes narrowed. "Yes. Speaking of unorthodox, where did you get that tie?"

Bryan glanced down at the tie, which featured Bugs Bunny on a snowboard. "My nephew gave it to me for Christmas," he said. "Do you like it?"

"No."

Bryan grinned. "I do." He checked his watch. "If you'll excuse me, I have to make some calls."

Leaving Carl looking dazed, Bryan strolled down the hall to his office. Zephyr was right. Taking a corporate job didn't mean he had to leave behind his old philosophy of living life on his own terms. He didn't have to let others dictate his decisions, whether they related to the clothes he wore, the way he interacted with others, or the woman he chose to love.

Chapter Fifteen

The sun streamed through the front windows of the Chocolate Moose, bathing the tables covered in tropical print fabric in a golden glow. A placard by the cash register announced a special on chocolate and banana smoothies and the whir of the mixer competed with the crooning of the Beach Boys on the loudspeaker. The stuffed moose head on the back wall wore sunglasses and a Colorado Rockies ball cap.

Angela added a cup of chopped peanuts to the peanut butter brownies she was mixing up and mentally reviewed the ingredients list for the brown sugar frosting she wanted to ice them with. She'd have to be sure to order more powdered sugar from her supplier.

"What does a customer have to do to get service around here?"

Smiling, Angela turned to greet Tanya. Dressed for summer in a white, sleeveless blouse and khaki walking shorts, sunglasses perched on top of her head and a straw bag over her arm, the director looked cool and sophisticated—the opposite of how Angela felt in her overheated kitchen. She shut off the mixer, untied her floral-print apron and hurried into the front room of the shop. "You look gorgeous, as usual," she said. "Want to try one of my smoothies?"

"That sounds really good." Tanya sat at one of the tables. "Do you have time to join me?"

"Let me put this batch of brownies in the oven and I can give you a few minutes." She started the smoothies whirring in the blender, then returned to the kitchen and spread the brownie batter in a pan.

Brownies in the oven, she poured the smoothies into a pair of parfait glasses and carried them to the table.

Tanya took a long pull at her straw. "That is so good," she said, closing her eyes in an expression of ecstasy.

"If one smoothie can make you that happy, I'd say you need to get out more," Angela said.

Tanya stuck out her tongue at her friend. "You're one to talk. But speaking of love lives, have you seen Bryan lately?"

Angela felt the familiar tightness in her chest any thought of Bryan always brought. "Not since dinner last Thursday." She sighed. "It's for the best."

"It is *not* for the best and you know it. You should call him."

Angela had lost track of how many times in the past four days she'd picked up the phone. "What could I say?" she asked.

"How about 'Bryan, I'm sorry. I didn't mean it when I said we shouldn't see each other. I was only scared of being hurt again. Will you give me another chance?'"

"Maybe I should have you call him for me?"

"Uh-uh." Tanya took another long sip of her drink. "Would you like me to repeat my little speech about having confidence in yourself?"

"Please, not the speech!" Angela stirred her drink with her straw. "I want to call him. I simply need a little more time to get my courage up. It's not the easiest thing in the world to admit to a guy you were wrong. And what if he's angry with me? What if he decides he's better off without me?"

"That's a risk you have to take, I guess."

Risk. Something she'd been thinking a lot about lately.

Tanya pushed away her empty glass. "Are you learning your lines for *The Red Lady's Revenge?*" she asked. "Do you need me to run through them with you?"

Auditions had been held Sunday afternoon and to Angela's surprise—and trepidation—Tanya had held to her pledge to award Angela the lead. "Sometime soon, maybe. I'm doing okay so far." She collected Tanya's empty glass and carried it and her own to the sink behind the counter.

"How much do I owe you?" Tanya asked, reaching for her purse.

"It's on the house. Thanks for convincing me to try out for the part of Roxanne."

"Didn't I tell you you'd be perfect?" Tanya stood and walked to the counter across from Angela. "Everybody was blown away by your performance. You were sexy and bold, with just the right touch of vulnerability. You were great."

"Thanks. This is a role that is really going to make me stretch—not like the comic sidekicks I usually play."

"We all need to get out of our comfort zones once in a while. To take a few risks."

There was that word again.

The string of sleigh bells attached to the front door jangled and the door opened, letting in the sounds of laughter and the throb of a motorcycle passing along Elk Avenue. Angela squinted through the glare at the man who stood on the threshold, wondering if her mind was playing tricks on her.

The seriousness of Bryan's steel gray summer-weight suit and sober expression was spoiled by the huge bouquet of paper flowers he carried. "Hello, Angela," he said. "Could I talk to you for a minute?"

"I was just leaving." Tanya gave Angela an encouraging look, snatched up her purse and scurried away.

Angela stared at Bryan, not trusting herself to speak. Her heart pounded and she felt light-headed.

"You look great," he said, moving a few steps toward her. "I've missed you."

She knew what she looked like, having caught a glimpse of her reflection in the mirror behind the front counter. Her hair was pulled back in a messy ponytail, stray strands curling around her face, and she had a streak of flour across one cheek. Her blue-flowered sundress was too tight across the chest and there was a smear of chocolate over her left breast. Proof positive that love was blind.

She sucked in a deep breath, realizing she'd stopped inhaling and exhaling pretty much since the door had opened. That explained the light-headedness. Now if she could only get past her sudden muteness.

"We need to talk," Bryan said.

Yes, they did. Still not speaking, she moved past him to the door, which she locked, then she flipped the sign to read Closed and pulled the shade. That still left the front window open for anyone to look into, but it at least gave the illusion of privacy. She smoothed the front of her dress, straightened her shoulders, and turned to face him. "Why paper flowers?" she asked.

He looked at the bouquet—bright orange zinnias, red roses, yellow daisies and something pink and fluffy. A dahlia, maybe? "The grocery store was out of fresh ones and won't have more until tomorrow. I didn't want to wait." He thrust them toward her. "I never got around to bringing you flowers before, so I wanted to now."

"Oh. Thank you." She took the bouquet and resisted the urge to stick her nose down in it. Of course they wouldn't smell like anything but paper, but it was such an instinctive gesture. And since her brain was functioning about as well as an engine with all the gears rusted, she was counting on instinct to get her through this encounter with Bryan.

His eyes met hers and the heat of his gaze shook her. All the passion and determination she'd admired in him was distilled in that gaze. "Why don't we sit?" she suggested. She wasn't sure how much longer her legs would support her, with him looking at her that way.

They sat opposite one another, the ridiculous bouquet of flowers resting on the table between them. "I've been thinking about what you said the last time we spoke," he said.

"I really shouldn't have said it," she blurted. "I've been meaning to—"

"No." The fierceness in that one word stopped her. "You were right about a lot of things. I had let my ambition blind me to lot of other important things." He frowned. "You made me see some things about myself that were pretty ugly."

She almost laughed; she imagined Bryan wasn't a man used to hearing that adjective applied to himself.

"I was just afraid of being hurt," she said. "I was projecting my own fears onto you."

"No. Zephyr said something similar, though I didn't want to hear it. The thing is—" He paused, as if searching for the right words. "I thought in order to make a good impression on my bosses, to get the promotions and raises I wanted, I had to make myself into the perfect corporate employee. I thought I could turn myself into that kind of guy and it wouldn't matter because in the end, I'd have what I wanted.

"It took me almost losing the most important things for me to wake up to how stupid I'd been."

He took her hand, and rubbed his thumb back and forth across her knuckles. "I don't want to be a corporate clone," he said. "I don't want to be anything but myself. If that means I don't climb the ladder as quickly as I'd like, so be it. I spent too many years living on my own terms to ever be happy with anything else."

"I've been doing some thinking, too," she said. "You know, it's funny. I've always thought of acting as a fun hobby, but this week I realized how long I'd made it my full-time occupation. For years, I've been playing the role of the strong, confident, independent woman. Being with you stripped away all that. You touched the real me who had been hiding behind that costume—the me who had never let go of a bunch of old insecurities and fears." His grip on her hand tightened, and she squeezed back, welcoming his silent support.

"I realized it was time to let go of that old me, and those old fears," she continued. "Maybe I'm not as strong as I pretended, but I want to be stronger. I want to take more risks, even if it means taking a chance on being hurt."

His eyes met hers once more, his gaze burning into her. "I won't hurt you," he said. "I love you. From the first day I met you, you made me feel things I've never felt about any other woman. I need you and want you and I don't care who knows it. To me, you're perfect." He stood and pulled her from her chair, into his arms, his mouth claiming hers in a kiss that left no room for argument.

When they finally broke the kiss, she couldn't keep back her smile. "I love you," she said. "I don't know why I let so many other feelings get in the way of that one."

"We're going to be happy together," he said. "Though I'm

counting on you to bring me to my senses if I ever let ambition be more important than friendship or love."

"We're going to be happy," she said. "I'll do my best to keep you in line."

They kissed again, sealing their pledge, as the Beach Boys sang about surfing and sports cars. "We make a good team," he said when they came up for air.

"We do." She smoothed the collar of his jacket. "You can be in charge of crunching numbers and planning parties, and I'll make sure everyone is fed and entertained."

"Are you planning our lives or a business?"

"Both. After all, you're going to need someone to run the restaurant side of your boutique hotel, aren't you?"

"Are you applying for the job?"

"I'm saying I'm interested—if you have an opening."

"I'll make one. I can't think of anyone who'd be more perfect for the position."

"Mmm." She kissed his cheek and closed her eyes, inhaling the lime-and-starch scent of him, mingled with the rich aroma of brownies baking. "One thing's for sure," she said.

"What's that?"

"If all else fails, we'll always have chocolate."

"Chocolate and each other. That's a promise."

The small, doubting part of her still shouted for her not to believe such a flimsy thing as a promise, but she silenced that voice with another kiss. Bryan wasn't Troy, and she wasn't the same woman she'd been even a week ago. She was willing to take a few more risks now. To try a new recipe for happily ever after—one whose sweetness and flavor would never fade.

* * * * *

Come back to Crested Butte!
Look for Cindi Myers's next book
THE DADDY AUDITION
Coming in July 2009 from Harlequin
American Romance

In honor of our 60th anniversary,
Harlequin® American Romance® is celebrating
by featuring an all-American male each month,
all year long with
MEN MADE IN AMERICA!
This June, we'll be featuring American men
living in the West.

Here's a sneak preview of
THE CHIEF RANGER by Rebecca Winters.

Chief Ranger Vance Rossiter has to confront the sister of a
man who died while under Vance's watch...and also
confront his attraction to her.

"Chief Ranger Rossiter?" The sight of the woman who'd stepped inside Vance's office brought him to his feet. "I'm Rachel Darrow. Your secretary said I should come right in."

"Please," he said, walking around his desk to shake her hand. At a glance he estimated she was in her mid-twenties. Her feminine curves did wonders for the pale blue T-shirt and jeans she was wearing. "Ranger Jarvis informed me there's a young boy with you."

The unfriendly expression in her beautiful green eyes caught him off guard. "Yes," was her clipped reply. "When we arrived in Yosemite the ranger told me I couldn't go anywhere in the park until I talked to you first."

"That's right."

"Knowing you wanted this meeting to be private, he offered to show my nephew around Headquarters."

So this woman was the victim's sister... "What's his name?"

"Nicky."

The boy who haunted Vance's dreams now had a name. "How old is he?"

"He turned six three weeks ago. Were you the man in charge when my brother and sister-in-law were killed?"

"Yes. To tell you I'm sorry for what happened couldn't begin to convey my feelings."

The woman's gaze didn't flicker. "I won't even try to describe mine. Just tell me one thing. Was their accident preventable?"

"Yes," he answered without hesitation.

"In other words, the people working under you fell asleep on your watch and two lives were snuffed out as a result."

Hearing it put like that, he had to set the record straight. "My staff had nothing to do with it. I, myself, could have prevented the loss of life."

Ms. Darrow's expression hardened. "So you admit culpability."

"Yes. I take full blame."

A look of pain crossed over her features. "You can just stand there and admit it?" Her cry echoed that of his own tortured soul.

"Yes." He sucked in his breath.

"I work for a cruise line. Aboard ship, it's the captain's responsibility to maintain rigid safety regulations. If a disaster like that had happened while he was in charge he would have been relieved of his command and never given another ship again."

Rachel Darrow couldn't know she was preaching to the converted. "If you've come to the park with the intention of bringing a lawsuit against me for negligence, maybe you should." It would only be what he deserved.

"Maybe I will."

In the next instant, she wheeled around and hurried out of his office. Vance could have gone after her, but it would cause a scene, something he was loath to do for a variety of reasons. In the first place, he needed to cool down before he approached her again.

The discovery of the Darrows' frozen bodies had affected every ranger in the park. A little boy had been orphaned—a boy whose aunt was all he had left.

* * * * *

Will Rachel allow Vance to explain—
and will she let him into her heart?
Find out in
THE CHIEF RANGER
Available June 2009
from Harlequin® American Romance®.

We'll be spotlighting a different series every month
throughout 2009 to celebrate our 60th anniversary.

Look for Harlequin®
American Romance® in June!

Join us for a year-long celebration of the rugged
American male! From cops to cowboys—
Men Made in America has the hero
you've been dreaming about!

Look for

The Chief Ranger

by Rebecca Winters, on sale in June!

REQUEST YOUR FREE BOOKS!
2 FREE NOVELS PLUS 2
FREE GIFTS!

Love, Home & Happiness!

YES! Please send me 2 FREE Harlequin® American Romance® novels and my 2 FREE gifts (gifts are worth about $10). After receiving them, if I don't wish to receive any more books, I can return the shipping statement marked "cancel." If I don't cancel, I will receive 4 brand-new novels every month and be billed just $4.24 per book in the U.S. or $4.99 per book in Canada.* That's a savings of close to 15% off the cover price! It's quite a bargain! Shipping and handling is just 50¢ per book. I understand that accepting the 2 free books and gifts places me under no obligation to buy anything. I can always return a shipment and cancel at any time. Even if I never buy another book from Harlequin, the two free books and gifts are mine to keep forever.

154 HDN EYSE   354 HDN EYSQ

Name	(PLEASE PRINT)	
Address		Apt. #
City	State/Prov.	Zip/Postal Code

Signature (if under 18, a parent or guardian must sign)

Mail to the Harlequin Reader Service:
IN U.S.A.: P.O. Box 1867, Buffalo, NY 14240-1867
IN CANADA: P.O. Box 609, Fort Erie, Ontario L2A 5X3

Not valid to current subscribers of Harlequin® American Romance® books.

Want to try two free books from another line?
Call 1-800-873-8635 or visit www.morefreebooks.com.

* Terms and prices subject to change without notice. Prices do not include applicable taxes. N.Y. residents add applicable sales tax. Canadian residents will be charged applicable provincial taxes and GST. Offer not valid in Quebec. This offer is limited to one order per household. All orders subject to approval. Credit or debit balances in a customer's account(s) may be offset by any other outstanding balance owed by or to the customer. Please allow 4 to 6 weeks for delivery. Offer available while quantities last.

Your Privacy: Harlequin is committed to protecting your privacy. Our Privacy Policy is available online at www.eHarlequin.com or upon request from the Reader Service. From time to time we make our lists of customers available to reputable third parties who may have a product or service of interest to you. If you would prefer we not share your name and address, please check here. ☐

HAR09R

HARLEQUIN® *Romance*®

Escape Around the World
Dream destinations, whirlwind weddings!

Honeymoon with the Boss
by
JESSICA HART

Top tycoon Tom Maddison is used to calling the shots—until his convenient marriage falls through. But rather than waste his honeymoon, he'll take his boardroom to the beach and bring his oh-so-sensible secretary Imogen on a tropical business trip! But will Tom finally see the sexy woman that prudent Imogen truly is?

Available in June wherever books are sold.

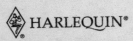

HARLEQUIN®

American ★ Romance®

COMING NEXT MONTH
Available June 9, 2009

#1261 THE CHIEF RANGER by Rebecca Winters
Men Made in America
As the chief ranger of Yosemite National Park, Vance Rossiter isn't surprised to be confronted by Rachel Darrow, a woman whose brother perished on El Capitan during a blizzard. It happened on his watch, he's to blame—and he'll do anything to make things right. Including taking Nicky, Rachel's orphaned nephew, under his wing. And educating Rachel about what really happened that fateful day…

#1262 MOMMY FOR HIRE by Cathy Gillen Thacker
Why Grady McCabe needs to buy a wife is a mystery to Alexis Graham. The attractive and wealthy developer isn't looking for love—only a mother for his little girl. Alexis can't imagine marrying for anything *but* love. Then when the matchmaking widow tries to change a certain Texan's mind, he starts to relent… and fall for *her!*
A special, bonus story from The McCabes of Texas miniseries!

#1263 THE TEXAS TWINS by Tina Leonard
When New York billionaire John Carruth came to No Chance, Texas, to save their rodeo from bankruptcy, he had no idea he'd be meeting his twin brother. Jake Fitzgerald, champion bull rider, didn't know he had another half. John may be kin, but he's still a stranger in these parts. It's a showdown between two rivals, to see which brother will win the woman of his dreams—and be the town's savior!
The Billionaire *and* The Bull Rider—*2 stories in 1!*

#1264 WAITING FOR BABY by Cathy McDavid
Baby To Be
Lilly Russo is thrilled—and terrified—to be pregnant. It's a bit of a shock that her brief affair with the owner of Bear Creek Ranch, Jake Tucker, led to a new life growing inside her. She's worried about being a mom, but she's even more concerned about Jake, already a busy single father of three girls. Can their relationship grow from a fling into love—considering there's a baby at stake?

www.eHarlequin.com

HARCNMBPA0509